"*Why do you want to go home?*" Léon asked

"Is it because you're homesick; or are you tired of Switzerland?"

"Because I must," Virginia replied. "Because of the wedding."

"The...wedding?" He shot her a startled sideways glance, but she didn't notice it. She was thinking of how he would be spending Christmas with Carla.

"When is this wedding to be?" he asked curtly.

"Early in January," she told him. Suddenly it struck her that Léon thought *she* was going to marry Clive, not her sister. Well, she decided, let him go ahead and think it. There was no reason why she shouldn't gather up the remnants of her pride and deceive him a little. Thank goodness for Clive who had made it possible for Léon to believe that she was not altogether unwanted!

Great love stories never grow old...

And we at Harlequin are proud to welcome you, our readers, to HARLEQUIN CLASSIC LIBRARY—a prime selection of time-tested, enduring favorites from the early lists of Harlequin's best-selling Romances.

Harlequin Romances have been read throughout the world for many years. Why? There are as many reasons as there are people. But longtime readers tell us that our books combine the enjoyment of travel, the intrigue of good plots, warm and interesting characters and the thrill of love. Each novel possesses an emotional appeal that sweeps you right into the wonderful world of romance!

As publishers of Harlequin Romances, we take a great deal of pride in our books. Since 1949 Harlequin has built its reputation on the solid base of quality and originality. And now our widely popular paperback romance novels have been translated into eighteen languages and are sold in more than eighty countries.

So...if you relish a classic love story, one whose appeal has lost nothing over the years, read the timeless Harlequin Romances in the HARLEQUIN CLASSIC LIBRARY. We hope you enjoy this story and all the others in our special selection of beautiful love stories from years past.

For a free catalogue of the books available, write to:
HARLEQUIN READER SERVICE
(In the U.S.) M.P.O. Box 707, Niagara Falls, N.Y. 14302
(In Canada) Stratford, Ontario, Canada   N5A 6W2

So Dear To My Heart

SUSAN BARRIE

Originally published as Harlequin Romance #572

HARLEQUIN
CLASSIC LIBRARY

TORONTO•LONDON•NEW YORK•AMSTERDAM
SYDNEY•HAMBURG•PARIS•STOCKHOLM

Original hardcover edition published by
Mills & Boon Limited 1956
ISBN 0-373-80006-1

Harlequin edition first published February 1961
Golden Harlequin Library edition, Volume XXXIX, published September 1973
Harlequin Classic Library edition published March 1980

CHAPTER ONE

WHEN THE TIME came for Virginia to say goodbye to Lisa in the wide cool hall where the smiling nurse looked on at them, it was as much as she could do to maintain her determinedly cheerful expression. Lisa looked so small, almost as if the tiredness resulting from the journey had caused her to shrink a little, and her dark eyes looked larger than ever in her wan, pinched face. But there was no sign of giving way to weakness or undergoing any change of mind about the set of her lips.

Virginia experienced a sudden tightness around her heart and her last words came in a rush.

"I'll come and see you tomorrow. And I'll bring you some magazines," she promised. "I'll be seeing Dr. Hanson in the morning but I expect they'll let me in to have a look at you in the afternoon."

"Have a good dinner tonight," Lisa said, smiling at her. "And wear your blue dress for the benefit of the other people in the dining room."

Virginia tried to smile back.

"I'm so tired I'll probably have something sent up to my room on a tray. But *you* must eat everything that's set in front of you! Good night, Liz."

Outside in the splendor of the evening she drove back to her hotel. It overlooked the lake, which had an appearance of unreality in the sunset light, with scarcely a ripple on its surface and a flawless sky above—a clear spring sky in which the first stars were already appearing. It reminded her of a drop scene at the theater, and despite her preoccupation with Lisa, when she had been whisked up in the elevator to her bedroom on the third floor, she stepped out onto her little balcony and continued to gaze at it all with admiration.

For, after London and Cromwell Road, it was something to give the heart a lift. At Heathrow Airport, when they had left, a cold rain had been falling and spring had seemed far behind. But here there was every evidence not only that it was well on its way but that summer was actually around the corner. A summer of alpine flowers and scents and indescribable sweetness. No hot dust or gasoline fumes or sidewalks retaining the heat of the day. Only the lake and the white-walled villas running down to its edge and the eternal snows capping the guardian chain of mountains.

Virginia lifted her eyes to the mountains and gripped the balcony rail. If only Lisa was all right! But she was *going* to be all right! Dr. Hanson would see to that....

Funny, Virginia thought, that they had had to come all the way from England to find a surgeon who could make life bearable again for Lisa.

She stared at the lake and recalled that the nurse had said that Dr. Hanson would see her in the morning. At eleven o'clock he would have a talk with her. And, presumably, he would also have a talk with Lisa before that hour arrived.

Virginia wished unreasonably that he could have made an exception in her case and see her tonight, if only for a few minutes, so that she could sleep and feel more assured in her own mind that Lisa was really in good hands and that whatever else happened nothing could go wrong with her. Although if the operation failed and Lisa had to return home with no comfort for her future, and with no promise that in time the ill effects of her accident would be completely wiped away and she would again play her piano, which had stood silent for so long—then life for Lisa would be the death-in-life she had been enduring for nearly ten months now and which so frightened all the members of her family.

For Lisa didn't simply take music seriously. It was her life. At fifteen she had made up her mind that the concert platform

was her aim, and at twenty-one she had stood firmly dedicated
to nothing else. Even her father and mother had recognized
that they had produced a musical genius in their younger
daughter. They had given her every encouragement and been
proud of the way she had worked—her acceptance of the fact
that it might be years before that dreamed-of first recital
which would set her on the road to success and give promi-
nence to the name of Lisa Holt. But as it happened those years
of painstaking devotion to only one object and that fanatical
disregard of all lesser pleasures and diversions had brought
their reward far earlier than had been expected, and Lisa's
first recital had been given and had attracted such favorable
notices that her future seemed assured. She was like a star that
would shoot across the sky with nothing in its path to stop it.
She was brilliant, she was remarkable, she was completely
happy!

Until the night when she was involved in a collison and the
taxi that was carrying her to her home on Cromwell Road
crumpled up like a concertina with Lisa inside it. And when
they knew that she would live they waited anxiously to learn
how soon, and how completely, she would recover. She did
recover the use of all her limbs, save her slender right hand,
which remained paralyzed. And a paralyzed right hand was a
hopeless right hand for a girl consumed by a burning ambition, a girl such as Lisa Holt.

At first the doctors suggested treatment, and one treatment
gave place to another, but without result. Lisa felt there was
little point in her having made a recovery at all if this was to
happen to her. If it had been her leg she could have borne
it—if it had been any part of her save her hand she could have
borne it!

Her eyes, which were naturally enormous, seemed to grow
lifeless in her face, and all their brown and youthful sparkle
might never have been. She had had a kind of elfin beauty that
had charmed when she had taken her place before a piano,
and the rippling movements of her fingers had delighted her

audiences; but now the beauty had become wan and faded and her tight little smile was full of bitterness. She had been cheated—so badly cheated that she felt she could not endure to go on unless some hope of some kind was sent to her to make existence bearable. And the hope was provided when a specialist pronounced his opinion that an operation performed by a certain Swiss surgeon might—and he would go so far as to say that he felt it was almost a certainty—restore life and flexibility to her fingers.

VIRGINIA RETURNED to her bedroom and slowly started to change her dress for dinner. Although she had said that she would have something on a tray she knew now that it would be impossible to spend the evening alone in that room with nothing but the vague noises of the hotel to distract her, the knowledge that she was in a country new and utterly strange to her to cast a kind of additional loneliness across her spirit, and the vision of Lisa's hollow-eyed face reappearing constantly before her eyes. And because Lisa had wished it she put on the blue dress that was her one and only evening gown. It had been bought for a tennis-club dance and suited her very well indeed.

Virginia had none of the striking, essentially vivid type of beauty that had once been her sister's. For one thing, she was four years older, although sometimes she actually looked much younger for her gray eyes were peculiarly guileless, and there was a gentle uncertainty about her smile. She was rather like a picture viewed through gauze, the tints subdued, the imperfections barely noticeable. Her skin had the pale flush of a drift of opening apple blossom; her brown hair looked as if it had been powdered with gold dust.

But her nose was not classically straight like Lisa's, and her mouth had a happy upward curve to the corners and found it difficult to compress itself into lines of determination or unshakable firmness.

She would not willingly have consented to go through all

that Lisa was willing to go through in order to realize an ambition. She was singularly without ambition, although, like most young women when the signpost of twenty has been left five years behind them, she did sometimes wonder a little about her future. She didn't dream dreams about her future, but she thought about it occasionally, and—wondered. . . .

Although Lisa was in a sense the invalid, it was she who had worked out all the details of this trip abroad—the first either of them had ever made unaccompanied by their parents—and who had insisted that Virginia stay at one of the best hotels, if only for a few days, until she could find less expensive accommodation. For less expensive accommodation was going to be essential when one took into account all the other mounting expenses that the unfortunate Mr. Holt had to meet on his younger daughter's account. The expense of the operation itself, in a country where there was no health service, as well as the support of his two daughters, since Virginia had had to give up her job as secretary in a lawyer's office in order to accompany her sister.

And then at home there were two younger brothers still at school. It was all rather a financial drain on the head of the family.

But if everything went well with Lisa, no one was going to raise any objections concerning this rather staggering expenditure that her health and her career had made necessary. Certainly not Virginia, who was going to remain near to her as long as it was at all possible and who had made up her mind to seek cheaper lodgings at the very earliest possible moment— just as soon as she had her talk with Dr. Hanson and her mind and her thoughts were at liberty to cope with less vital matters.

She was intensely conscious of her strangeness and her isolation in that spendid hotel when she descended to the brilliantly lighted lounge where, despite the fact that it was out of season, a large number of people seemed to be enjoying the many amenities. They were such smartly dressed people, too—especially the Americans, whose voices mingled with the

flow of continental tongues around her, and gave her a feeling
of confidence because they were after all speaking her own
language.

A waiter found her a small table for one in the dining room
and Virginia sank gratefully onto the chair he pulled out for
her, thankful for the protection of a huge palm in an ornamental brass-banded tub beside her.

The waiter understood English far better than she was able
to express herself in her schoolgirl French, and she colored
rather delightfully when he smiled and suggested, with
scarcely any accent at all, items on the menu that he thought
would be likely to appeal to her. Although she did not realize
it, the blue dress—deep, midnight-blue georgette with a finely
pleated skirt—worn with a tiny bolero of silver brocade, made
the most of her typically English fairness, and combined with
the shy charm of her smile it was sufficient to set her a little
apart from the rest. Even the waiter found the task of looking
after her a pleasant one.

At a table close to her a party of four people had just taken
their seats and from the extreme deference of the waiter
attending to them—to say nothing of the bows and smiles of
the maître d'hotel from the moment they appeared in the
dining room—they were visitors of distinction whose patron-
age was much appreciated.

From where she sat beside the palm Virginia could study
them without being observed herself and she noticed that of
the two women one was quite spectacularly lovely, wearing a
confection that breathed Paris in every line, while of the two
men the younger had grave good looks that made him a most
fitting escort for his exotic companion. She directed her smiles
brilliantly at him and Virginia was almost dazzled by the
perfection of her milky even teeth and the spun-gold wonder
of her hair, which was wound in a coronet of braids about her
regally poised head.

A fascinating display of jewelry winked at her ears and
about her rounded throat and arms, and that it was costly

jewelry Virginia never had a doubt. One had only to look at the dark, slightly austere face of the man with the sleek head who bent toward her—the chiseled perfection of the straight nose and the mouth and the clearly defined jaw made the English girl think of fine pieces of sculpture she had seen—and to recognize his attentiveness, and the fastidious attention to detail where his own grooming was concerned, to be very sure of that. And the elderly couple who made up the party looked opulent and expansive, but just as unmistakably well bred.

Virginia wondered whether the young, attractive couple was an engaged couple, with the older pair being the parents of the girl. This might easily have been the case, judging by the almost fond looks the elderly pair bestowed on the young woman and the interested manner in which they occasionally studied the young man.

Virginia noticed that champagne in an ice bucket had been brought to their table; they seemed to be having some kind of a celebration. Was it an engagement party, she wondered.

As soon as she had finished her dinner she rose with the intention of spending half an hour in the lounge before retiring to bed. As she neared the tall swinging doors a couple of athletic blond young men, who looked as if mountain climbing might be among their hobbies, walked carelessly through them. Without noticing her approach one of them let the door through which she was about to pass swing back in her face, so that it caught her a glancing blow on one side of her head that caused all the lights in the dining room to whirl madly around her for a moment, while she clung to the handle for temporary support.

The blond young man who had inflicted the punishment uttered a guttural exclamation and looked horrified. His companion, more practical, inquired anxiously whether she was hurt.

"We did not see you, *Fräulein!*" he exclaimed, his German accent very noticeable. "And my friend here is of a clumsiness to be despised! I trust that you are not hurt—?"

"No; only a little—a little dizzy!" Virginia answered, trying to smile and make light of the incident, although she was feeling almost deathly sick; she had gone very white and was still clinging to the handle of the door. "I—I'll be all right in a minute. I'll take a seat in the lounge—"

"Here—take my arm," said the concerned giant, offering it somewhat belatedly; but he was firmly put aside by the grave-faced, dark-haired young man who had been dining at the table close to Virginia's own, and who did not wait to offer her his arm but put it around her and guided her to a discreetly placed couch just inside the door. He sat down beside her as she collapsed rather weakly onto the cushions, and putting out a hand encircled her wrist with his fingers and looked keenly into her face.

"I'm afraid that the door hit you on the head, did it not?" he asked, his voice very quiet and almost as English as her own.

Somehow the feel of his firm fingers around her wrist was as soothing as a sedative to her just then, and whether it was his touch or some quality in his voice that acted like a stimulant, as well, she was unable to decide. She did know, however, that the lights all at once stopped whirling, her inside stopped being revolted, and the color swept back into her cheeks in a rush as she said, "But it was my own fault! I—I should have looked where I was going." Actually she had been wondering whether there would be many people in the lounge and whether much of their attention would be diverted to her, alone and unattended in such a big hotel. "The young man was not to blame. Really, he wasn't—"

But the young man was bowing in front of her and apologizing afresh in a flood of mixed German and English. He looked very red and uncomfortable and his friend, who was standing beside him, looked just as red and just as uncomfortable. The dark man beside Virginia on the couch ignored them, however, and stretching forth his hand received something from a waiter who had not wasted any time. Virginia found that she was expected to dispose of a small glass of something that looked and smelled like neat alcohol. She hesitated, received an order to "Drink it up!" and obeyed—choking over it a little —and then felt surprisingly much better than she had felt before.

"Good girl!" exclaimed the quiet voice beside her. He ceased holding her wrist and began to run his fingers lightly through her hair, feeling for the bump that had already risen under the soft brown curls. He looked at her with a little smile in his eyes. "I'm afraid it is going to be rather painful for a day or two, but it will subside quite soon. I will send some stuff up to you that, if you follow the instructions and paint it over the bruise, will help to mend matters even more quickly. And now I think you would be wise if you went up to your room."

"Yes," Virginia said, adding meekly, "I will."

"You'll feel better in the morning."

"I hope so," she murmured.

"You feel better already, don't you?" he asked, raking her with that keen look.

"Much better," she admitted.

She realized that she was not being very bright, but although she was almost completely restored to normal there was something about the whole affair, coming as it did on the top of a day devoted to travel and emotional upheaval, that had shaken her right out of her natural composure. And with his dark eyes resting on her—so reassuring and yet so inscrutable, so strangely penetrating and yet kindly and understanding at the same time, she felt as if her wits had temporarily deserted her and speech simply would not come easily.

"If you like I'll take you up to your room?"

"No, thank you," she answered. "I can manage."

She was about to add thanks for his prompt attention— dimly it occurred to her that he must be a doctor or at least he was capable of dealing with an emergency such as the one she had presented him with—when a shadow glided gracefully in front of them and a voice as delectable as ice-cooled wine inquired softly, "Is there anything I can do? Is your patient responding to treatment, Léon?"

Virginia looked up at her vaguely. She recognized the slim form, the expensive and cloudy gown of black net scattered like stardust with sequins, and the gold-crowned head above it. She remembered that she had sat studying this woman with interest while she was eating her dinner. But now that the clear eyes of extraordinarily deep and translucent blue were looking directly at her they confused her a little and she began to stammer awkwardly, "Thank you, I—I'm quite all right now! It was just an accident. I—I'll go upstairs to my room, if—if you would be so good as to direct me to the elevator?"

"Of course," the man responded immediately, and rising, he assisted her to her feet. He kept a firm hold of her arm as she took her first steps away from the settee. She still felt a little wobbly about the knees but she resisted the temptation to make an impulsive, clutching movement at his black-clad arm.

"And you're quite sure there's nothing I can do?"

It was the young woman again—the young woman with the startling blue eyes that were smiling at Virginia almost too sweetly but without any real concern.

"Nothing," her dinner companion assured her, and guided Virginia in the direction of the elevator. "Thanks, Carla."

"Then don't be long, Léon," she called after him. "Remember that we haven't a great deal of time if we're going on to the Van Loons'."

Her eyes ceased to smile the instant Virginia's back was turned to her, but the waiter who was hovering near attracted her notice and she addressed him with a tiny, petulant frown between her slender, arched brows, while the original blond culprit escaped to the dining room with his companion.

"Such appalling clumsiness!" she exclaimed, in biting and penetrating accents that could not fail to reach the ears of the departing offender. "A couple of hooligans, surely?"

Whereupon the unfortunate young German's ears turned redder than ever and his friend dragged him to a table in a corner, screened by a palm in a brass-bound tub—which was actually the table at which Virginia herself had sat.

In the entrance to the elevator Virginia looked once more into the grave dark eyes of the man who was waiting to say good night to her and she shyly tried to thank him.

"You were most kind," she said.

"Not at all," he answered. "It was an unfortunate accident."

The elevator carried her to her bedroom on the third floor. Once inside the room her weariness crowded upon her as if it was something physical that was seeking to crush her, and her head started to ache abominably. She undressed without thinking coherently of anything whatsoever and tumbled into bed at last with a sensation of vast relief. It was a bed that was much too large for her but so deliciously soft and comfortable that she fell asleep immediately without even remembering to turn off the light.

CHAPTER TWO

IN THE MORNING, very much to her annoyance, Virginia slept late, and instead of the pleasant hour looking at new and strange shops filled with intriguing but costly trifles far beyond the reach of her limited purse strings, which friends had warned her to expect, but which she had promised herself the evening before, she had to dash off to keep her appointment with Dr. Hanson without even waiting for a cup of coffee. She had intended to buy Lisa something rather captivating in the bed-jacket line, as well as the magazines she had promised her, but they would have to wait now.

Dr. Hanson's house had an austerity about its furnishings that was more or less what she had expected, but there were bowls of flowers in his waiting room and she admired his taste in watercolors very much indeed. They lent a touch of color to the severe white walls and some blue delft china on a dark oak dresser looked homey and attractive.

She was admitted by a maid and then interviewed by a secretary who conducted her to Dr. Hanson's consulting room. He was seated at a desk when she entered and he did not look up immediately, but the secretary pulled up a chair for her.

She did not sit down but remained rooted to the floor, so overcome by surprise that she almost allowed it to pass her lips. She nearly said, as he looked up slowly at last and surveyed her with his quiet eyes, "You!"

He smiled at her slightly.

"Sit down, Miss Holt." His English was certainly almost faultless. He did not offer to shake hands with her but rose and stood behind his desk until he saw that she was comfortably seated. "How is the head this morning?"

"Oh better—much better." Her astonishment was passing but the sense of confusion it had brought with it remained for a brief while longer. "That is to say, it's a bit tender still—" putting her fingers rather gingerly to the lump that had made it impossible to wear a hat "—and it hurts when I touch it. But I slept so well last night that I made myself late this morning and I really haven't thought very much about it."

"Good," he said. "It was a nasty knock you received but I said you would feel better this morning, didn't I?"

Actually he thought she was looking remarkably fresh in her neat spring suit with a little blouse of palest daffodil yellow that had its tiny collar turned down over the suit. The sunlight that was streaming into his room found all the golden lights in her hair and her complexion was something to marvel at in the broad, clear light of day. She had a shy look in her gray eyes that made them peculiarly attractive.

"You're wondering whether I knew who you were last night, aren't you?" he said at last, smiling again. "Well, I didn't at the time but I found out afterward at the reception desk." He passed a silver cigarette box across to her and then leaned across the desk to hold the end of his lighter to her cigarette. She thought that his dark eyes had an amused look in them. "You're younger than your sister, aren't you, Miss Holt?"

"Why, no," she answered. "Actually I'm nearly four years older. But Lisa does sometimes look a little—well, she takes life rather seriously, for one thing, and since her accident she hasn't been too happy...."

That was a vast understatement but at least it brought Lisa forward into the picture without any more delay, and her heart was knocking with anxiety to learn what he thought were the chances of her much-loved younger sister. She hardly dared to ask him but he could see from her expression what her thoughts were. His face became suddenly grave and thoughtful and he stared down at the top of his desk where a little pile of neatly typewritten letters awaited his signature.

He picked up his fountain pen and toyed with it for a moment and she could see that his hands were beautiful—beautifully formed and cared for with sensitive tips to the long fingers. His wrists beneath his immaculate cuffs had a look of strength and virility about them.

"Miss Lisa, I take it, has ambitions as a concert pianist?" he said.

"She *had* ambitions," Virginia replied quietly.

He still stared at the desk.

"And if those ambitions are not realized, is she, do you think, the type to refuse to consider any other sort of a career or any other kind of life that does not include music? Is music her whole life or do you think in time she might become reconciled to listening to it rather than creating it? She is young. There is every possibility that she will marry one day—"

"I don't think Lisa would ever regard marriage as a compensation she could accept instead of a musical career," Virginia told him slowly and quite honestly.

"Don't you?" He looked at her suddenly, keenly. "Is your family ambitious, Miss Holt? Is it, perhaps, in the blood?"

"Oh, no, I'm sure it isn't." A faint pink invaded her cheeks as she felt him studying her. "As a family we are not in the least brilliant and I think that is why we are all so proud of Lisa, so terribly proud!" Her eyes sought his. "Is there any hope for her, Dr. Hanson? Will she—will she play again? If you decide to operate, that is?"

"I will be quite frank with you, Miss Holt." He lighted himself another cigarette although hers was smoldering almost unheeded between her fingers. "I am quite sure that I can restore to your sister the almost complete use of her right hand. So little doubt is there of that that I do not even say 'if she is willing to take the risk.' But whether I can restore to her the flexibility in her fingers that in time will turn her into a prominent pianist is another matter. Almost certainly she will play again—well enough to make a first-class teacher of music, if necessary! But to be a teacher of music is not the niche she has carved out for herself in her imagination, is it? It is not what you all have hoped for her?"

Virginia admitted with a cold feeling at her heart that it most certainly was not. The hopes of the family had been boundless where Lisa was concerned and even now they still hoped.... And it was hope, and hope alone, that was at the back of Lisa's fortitude, the reason why she was prepared to undergo almost anything if it held out the promise of the future she had planned. But if there was no real chance of its ever being given back to her ....

Virginia tried to explain to Dr. Hanson the way Lisa felt about things, with her intense nature and her inability to do by halves anything she wished to do. The way she allowed herself to be consumed by her ambition. If she ever fell in love—and she might do so one day, Virginia thought—then it would be a love that would consume her just as her ambition consumed her and would certainly not be denied. It would sweep all before it—even, perhaps, those things now nearest to her heart—and any slight difficulties in the way of its fulfillment would be regarded as no difficulties at all by Lisa. For that was the way she was made. An enormously powerful spirit in a slight and rather fragile body that was inclined to mislead some people. It might even have misled Dr. Hanson although he listened with attention to all that Virginia thought it necessary to tell him about her sister, and when her voice wandered off—when she realized that there was little more she could say to put Lisa's side of her unhappy story more clearly to him—she was by no means certain that he was entirely sympathetic, for his voice and his expression gave away nothing at all.

She realized that in the life he led he must come upon cases of even greater hardship and frustration than Lisa's. For Lisa, after all, had not only survived her accident, but was comparatively whole again, even if she could no longer pursue her chosen career. But he must surely recognize that Lisa was young—she had every *right* to expect much of life, and the fact that she was so plucky about everything should surely earn her his esteem?

And Lisa as a teacher of music, when she had hoped to delight vast audiences? Oh, *no*, thought Virginia.

"And there is no more hope than that?" she asked at last with rather a shaky note in her voice.

"Yes," he replied instantly, to her surprise, "there is! But I thought it best that you should have the true picture of the case put before you. At worst your sister will regain the use of her right hand and arm, which at the moment are practically paralyzed; such use, I mean as any ordinary person would have. At best she will regain the fullest use of the fingers of her right hand and that will mean that she can go ahead with her career —after exercises, of course, to strengthen the fingers and render them supple again."

"Oh!" Virginia exclaimed and her eyes began to shine.

"*But*," he said with emphasis on the word, "at the moment she is far too tense and strung up to make success, even on a moderate scale, at all likely, if I operate at once. She is like a violin string that is too taut. She must be made to relax, and with that object in view I propose keeping her at the clinic for a week or two until I can judge the effect that complete physical, if not mental, rest and relaxation have had on her. And the effect of the air here should prove beneficial in her case, also."

Virginia felt her heart sink again. They had hoped that the operation would be soon, cutting down the expense and the length of their visit. But if it was important to Lisa . . . .

"You will remain near her?" Dr. Hanson asked, studying her face in that unconcealed fashion that made her feel more than a little embarrassed. She found it difficult to meet his eyes all the time because they affected her with the odd belief that it was a comparatively simple matter for him to read all the secrets that dwelt behind her own gray eyes.

"Oh, yes," she answered at once. "I must. I promised her, and in any case I couldn't bear to leave her . . . ."

"Then you will stay on at the hotel?"

She shook her head. "That would be too expensive. I shall have to find somewhere cheaper."

"I see," he said. He appeared to consult a calendar on his desk and then he looked up at her again. "In that case I might be able to help you—if you would like me to do so?"

She assured him that she would be more than grateful. "I'm a stranger in a strange land," she said. She laughed a little ruefully. "I don't even understand the language."

He regarded her with an odd, cool smile in his eyes. "I'm sure you speak schoolgirl French well enough," he told her, and stood up. "If you'll forgive me, Miss Holt, I have a very busy morning ahead of me, and there is not much more we have to talk about at the present time. But if I can give you a lift back to your hotel I will."

"Thank you," she said. She felt a little abashed by his abrupt method of terminating the interview; but when they went out to his car, standing long and sleek and black in front of his house, and he opened the door for her to sit beside him, he repeated his willingness to help her in the matter of finding accommodation more suited to her pocket than the hotel at which she was presently staying, and she again thanked him.

"In the meantime," he said, "you must do your best to keep your sister cheerful and it will be as well if you do not let her know that there is any doubt at all about the absolute success of the operation when I decide to perform it."

BUT LISA, when Virginia saw her that afternoon, reflected in her enormous eyes the question that had been making her feel restless all day, even before she uttered it with her lips.

"Have you seen Dr. Hanson? And what did he say to you, Jinny?"

Virginia sank down in a long cane chair, which was placed beside Lisa's on a veranda that overlooked the lake, and onto which her quite pleasantly furnished bedroom opened. For a moment Virginia was so entranced by the beauty of the lake that she did not answer. The whole panorama still made her think of a drop scene at the theater, but this afternoon there was a faint haze over the water and the sun was shining as through a curtain of gauze. The sky was a tender, tranquil blue and there were one or two unreal clouds drifting across it. She thought, "A blue sky of spring, white clouds on the wing. . . ."

"Well?" Lisa insisted. "What did he say?"

Virginia decided to be truthful, up to a point.

"That you've got to be a good girl and stop worrying about all this and relax. It's no good, Lisa! You can't expect any man to give you back the use of your hands if you won't help him a little by unwinding yourself at least a bit. He says you're like a violin string and you've got to let yourself go. You must try to do that, Liz."

"Hmm!" Lisa exclaimed. "He did make some remark of a similar kind to me when he came to see me after breakfast this morning. At least he said I was not to worry and that I was to make the most of my stay here because this is a wonderful part of the world in spring. Instead of examining me he talked a lot about the flowers and how soon the snow vanishes from the valleys and what it's like here in summer. He's very fond of his own country, I must say, and he seems very self-assured."

"I suppose most surgeons are self-assured," Virginia said. "Otherwise other people wouldn't have confidence in them."

"No," Lisa agreed with a shadow crossing her face. "One does have to entrust rather a lot to them, doesn't one?"

Virginia decided to change the subject.

"Anyway," she said, "You're looking much better. You've actually got a spot of color in your cheeks, and lying there like that all tucked up in that camel's-hair rug you appear really luxurious."

Lisa smiled at her.

"I've been told that I've got to be very lazy for the next day or so," she said, "and the air here is so much like champagne that it would be a poor complexion that didn't perk up a little after a morning spent on this balcony." And then, determinedly, she returned to the question that interested her. "Did Dr. Hanson say anything else to you, Jinny?"

"No, darling, nothing of any importance." Virginia stretched herself in her chair and appeared to be enjoying the sunshine. "He's satisfied that he can get your fingers to work if you cooperate by forgetting everything and making the most of the weeks that you've got to stay here."

"Weeks?" Lisa exclaimed, aghast.

"Yes, darling, two or three. And I must say you could hardly be in a nicer spot."

"But what about you?" Lisa asked. "Will you be able to afford to stay at that hotel all that time? Why, we were planning to return to England in not much more than two weeks!"

"I know," Virginia answered. "But I've got all that in hand and I'll look for somewhere cheaper. I might even manage to get taken in by a Swiss family. That would be a good deal pleasanter than a hotel."

She decided not to tell Lisa about Dr. Hanson's half promise to find her somewhere else to stay in case by some chance he couldn't help her—for whatever happened Lisa must have her belief in him kept well and truly buoyed up. Nor would she tell her sister about the little incident of her bump on the head the night before. Lisa was inclined to worry over things like that. She would worry about Virginia, alone and unprotected in a strange hotel and although she was the elder of the two, lacking Lisa's calm confidence and composure when making contact with fresh faces and unexplored situations.

As if she had the power to read Virginia's thoughts, Lisa looked at her affectionately and observed suddenly, "Poor old Jinny! I don't like to think of you all on your own and without anyone to talk to."

"Then don't think," Virginia advised. "It isn't necessary."

"But you'll find it so dull. And although the hotel's expensive I'd rather think of you there than hunting around looking for doubtful lodgings. You're not the type, somehow."

"You mean that I have a helpless streak in me? Or you imagine I have!"

"No, it's not that. But you look helpless."

"Thank you," with an amused smile in her eyes.

"You're the feminine type—the ultrafeminine type! And you're too pretty."

"Goodness!" Virginia exclaimed. "You amaze me! I've always thought of myself as passably plain."

Lisa studied her. "You're the sort of woman James Barrie had in mind when he wrote *Quality Street*. Someday some man will want to liken you to a garden and wrap you up in cotton wool."

"Then he'll have to be fairly expeditious," Virginia said "because I was twenty-five on my last birthday, and in *Quality Street* that would place me high up on the shelf."

"You suggest ringlets and lavender and a quiet background," Lisa persisted. "You weren't meant for the rough and tumble."

"There's no rough and tumble about the hotel in which I'm staying at the present time, I can assure you," Virginia told her, thinking of the elegance of the young woman who had been with Dr. Hanson the night before. And she had called him Léon! "It is absolutely super, as Jinx would say." Jinx was their youngest schoolboy brother.

When she left Lisa was beginning to delve into the volume of Swiss fairy tales, (translated into English), that Virginia had unearthed for her in a bookshop, and with a supply of magazines to last her until the sisters saw each other again, which Virginia promised would be the following afternoon. She was satisfied because the color in Lisa's cheeks was in no way due to makeup and she seemed somehow resigned—which was better than being overacutely aware of what awaited her and what might or might not be awaiting her in her future.

CHAPTER THREE

TWO DAYS LATER Virginia received a telephone call at her hotel from Dr. Hanson, who said he would like to see her. When she suggested paying another visit to his consulting room he replied that he would prefer to talk to her in the hotel lounge, if that was convenient for her, and as it was the afternoon tea hour she sat waiting for him at a little table in a corner with a waiter ready to serve them tea as soon as the doctor arrived.

He came in looking as impeccably groomed as she remembered, him but with his dark eyes even darker than she remembered, and that black, sleek hair of his dipping into the merest suggestion of a wave over one well-marked eyebrow. Virginia had gone out shopping that morning and had been unable to withstand the temptation to buy herself one of the dainty, embroidered muslin blouses that were so popular in that part of the world—although far more expensive than she could afford—and she was wearing it with a finely pleated skirt and a little mist-blue cardigan that was draped across her shoulders. Her hair had received a fresh set, too, from a Swiss hairdresser—it was shining like a polished chestnut in the dim corner of the lounge.

Dr. Hanson accepted tea—although she was not sure that it was one of his daily habits—and sat looking at her for a few moments in silence before he explained to her what it was that he wished to see her about.

"I want you to know that I have arranged for you to stay in a more suitable place than this," he told her then, as if it were quite impossible that she could have any objection to falling in with the arrangement. "I think you will be much happier, and your sister will probably be easier in her mind because you are well looked after, and altogether it is quite an excellent arrangement."

"Oh?" Virginia said in faint astonishment, waiting for him to explain the arrangement he had made. But he produced his cigarette case, handed it to her and carefully lighted her cigarette and his own before proceeding to enlighten her.

"My aunt will be delighted to have you as her guest," he told her, almost taking her breath away completely by the statement. "She lives in a house that is much too large for her and she is a little lonely sometimes because she no longer entertains as much as it was once her custom to do. She has always been particularly devoted to young people, so you will be bestowing a kindness if you remain with her until the time arrives when you can return with your sister to England."

"Oh, but—" Virginia wondered whether she could have heard correctly "—I couldn't possibly take advantage of such a kind offer! Why, your aunt hasn't even met me!"

"True," he agreed with an eyebrow raised in surprise. "But is that any reason why you shouldn't stay with her? As I have already explained, she will be delighted to have you and unless you have already made plans for yourself—"

"Oh, no," she assured him. "I haven't made any plans at all."

"Then you have perhaps an objection to staying with my aunt?"

"Certainly not!" she exclaimed, her voice quite warm with indignation because she felt that he was willfully misunderstanding her. "I think it is tremendously good of your aunt and—oh, but don't you see—" She spread her hands a little and an earnest pink flush invaded her cheeks. "I can't possibly take advantage of such—such an offer when I'm a complete stranger...."

"Yes, I do see," he told her, a rather cool note in his voice and an amused gleam in his dark eyes as he regarded her. "You English have a perfect passion for being independent, haven't you? And although if you persist in being independent it may mean that your sister, who has need of you, may have to be left alone here without any of her own people near her at a time when her morale needs to be bolstered, you would rather that that should happen than that you should accept the hospitality of a relative of mine who would be only too happy to have you beneath her roof. Well, in that case—"

But Virginia's color had risen wildly, and she made a quick effort to soften what she realized must have looked a little like ungraciousness.

"Oh, no!" she said. "I would do anything to remain near Lisa! It's only that the suggestion that I stay with your aunt took me very much by surprise."

"Then, having overcome your surprise you are willing to consider the idea?" There was a slightly softer note in his voice and his eyes twinkled a little. "Perhaps if I take you along to see her, and you two have a talk—what then? Aunt Héloïse may be able to persuade you, having, we will trust, a greater power of overcoming your scruples."

She felt that he was laughing at her a little, but he stood up now as if he had firmly made up his mind that she could not refuse to meet his relative. She stood up, also, but still a little hesitantly. He might have a quiet voice and a quiet manner, but there was something so incisive, even slightly implacable about him at times, that she felt it would be unpleasant to be involved in a really serious argument with him. And, in any case, she had a feeling already that he would win, whatever the argument.

"But I don't feel I have a right to take up so much of your time," she said.

"Nonsense!" he exclaimed. "This afternoon I am able to spare the time, so we will go at once if you are ready."

She did not even leave him to fetch a hat as he was striding ahead of her through the hotel lounge, which was packed at that hour with a considerable number of visitors; and when they were outside he helped her into his long black car and got in beside her at the wheel. She wondered whether he always drove himself or whether there were occasions when he made use of the services of a chauffeur; but his hands looked so flexible and virile on the wheel that they quite fascinated her and she realized that he probably enjoyed driving. In any case it was a most luxurious car and it threaded its way among the traffic on the lakeshore with a soundlessness and ease that conveyed an impression that it was propelled by magic.

Virginia forgot after a time, however, to study his hands because the beauty of the lake compelled her to lift her eyes to it. The snow on the mountain peaks was at its most dazzling and slightly unearthly point of perfection at this hour, with the gold of the sun already declining. The gardens of the villas that dreamed on the shore of the lake were all a wilderness of blossom, purple and white lilac and clematis, pink chestnut and alpine roses. Orchards spread like a sea of pink and white foam almost overhanging the crystal clear water, and the deep green of new leaves was restful by comparison.

"Have you made up your mind yet whether you like it here?" Dr. Hanson asked her suddenly, when they had been driving in silence for several minutes.

"Oh, yes," Virginia answered at once. "I think it's almost too beautiful. And everything looks so extraordinarily clean," she added with a little laugh, "as if all the shops and houses were washed clean every morning by some magic dew!" "But I expect it's probably something to do with the atmosphere."

"This is your first visit to Switzerland?"

"Yes. As a family we are not travelers. I suppose because we've never been able to afford it," she replied candidly.

He gave her a curious side glance and then looked away. "As a family you are at least united," he observed.

He slowed the car to permit her to admire one of the most enchanting gardens on the shore of the lake, with a white house like a miniature palace in a fairy tale crowning the heights above it. A boat was moored to some timeworn steps that led into the pellucid waters of the lake.

"That is the home of the Van Loons," he said. "They are friends of mine, very charming American friends."

And Virginia recalled that on the night when she had first made his acquaintance in the dining room of her hotel, his lovely feminine companion, Carla, had reminded him that they were going on to the Van Loons'. She wondered what sort of evening they had had there together.

Aunt Héloise, or Madame d'Auvergne, was seated in a room that made Virginia think of a grand salon when she and Dr. Hanson entered it together. All her preconceived notions of what a villa should look like, which had been built up largely on a study of advertisements in local newspapers at home announcing, often ambiguously, "a villa at Ealing," or Twickenham or some such district, accompanied by a photograph that had often impressed her, were upset entirely by both the outside and the inside of Madame d'Auvergne's villa.

It was not as large as the Van Loons' and not quite as fairylike, but it was a place to delight the most aesthetic taste. The salon, where the mistress of the place awaited them in a wide window that overlooked all the exotic delights of the garden, was not only of splendid proportions but exquisitely furnished. And Aunt Héloise herself looked like a grand duchess with high-piled white hair and a complexion that was a challenge to every young woman of her acquaintance. She was dressed as if about to receive the most important company in something that looked like a robe of dove-gray velvet. On her breast were pinned more than one glittering brooch and there were several rows of pearls about her neck.

"So there you are, my dear!" she exclaimed upon meeting Virginia. She smiled and leaned forward, one hand on a slender ebony cane, but did not rise or come to meet them. Later Virginia was to discover that she was a martyr to rheumatism that even her nephew could not cure.

But just now her expression was smiling and beaming and there was a kind of sparkling gaiety in her voice. "How nice," she said, "how *very* nice that Léon was able to persuade you!

hope you've brought all your things with you, my dear? There's no need for you to go back to the hotel at all."

Virginia felt Dr. Hanson's eyes on her, a somewhat sardonic gleam in them.

"First, my dear aunt," he said, "you have to convince Miss Holt that she is really welcome, that she is not inconveniencing you in the very smallest degree. *And* I think also that she has the Englishwoman's horror of not being quite independent, which you will have to do something about!"

"Tut, tut!" exclaimed his aunt. "We will see about that." She looked at Virginia as if she found her a most pleasing spectacle to gaze at. "What pretty hair you have, my dear," she told her. "It reminds me very much of what my own was like before it turned so uncompromisingly white!"

She touched a little bell at her elbow. "We will have tea and a talk and you and I will get to know one another. Léon can run away to his patients or to anyone else whom he might care to run to, but it is essential to our becoming acquainted that he should not be around while we do so."

Léon Hanson smiled in a way that Virginia had already discovered he could do—charmingly, with a flash of very even white teeth. It was a smile that had obvious affection in it as his eyes dwelt on Madame d'Auvergne.

"I accept my dismissal with equanimity," he told her. "But Miss Holt has already consumed one lot of tea this afternoon, although I don't suppose she'll be averse to another. Englishwomen get a great deal of consolation out of endless cups of tea." He looked at Virginia with a faint challenge in his eyes. "Shall I have your cases sent here to you, Miss Holt? If you like I will settle with the proprietor and you can settle with me later."

"Thank you," Virginia answered, realizing that she would appear ungracious indeed if she still declined to accept Madame d'Auvergne's hospitality. "That would be kind of you."

Aunt Héloïse regarded her nephew triumphantly. "So I succeed where you failed, Léon."

"Apparently," he answered, a faintly dry note in his voice.

And then they all looked up as a car swept up to the foot of the terrace steps and a slender and very elegant young woman stepped out and moved toward the glassed-in front porch.

"Ah, that is Carla come to say goodbye!" Aunt Héloise exclaimed. She looked toward Virginia and explained, "Carla has a voice—a voice like a bird—and she is going to Italy to sing at La Scala. And after that she pays a short visit to America."

But Virginia was watching Léon Hanson. He was standing near the window and had been studying every graceful movement of the woman who had come to say goodbye. And his face was dark—dark and plunged into a kind of inscrutable gloom that had in it a curious, forbidding quality.

She remembered that he had not seemed particularly sympathetic about Lisa's interrupted musical career. Was it because the very thought of a young woman following the profession of music was painful to him at this time? Perhaps intensely painful!

CHAPTER FOUR

DURING THE NEXT few days Virginia found it was quite a simple matter to settle down comfortably as an obviously welcome guest in Madame d'Auvergne's household. Madame d'Auvergne was the ideal hostess and as a lover of luxury in her own surroundings, she saw to it that visitors beneath her roof enjoyed to the full its many amenities.

Virginia was provided with a bedroom that was far more luxurious than anything she had ever slept in. When she first saw it she could hardly believe it was to be placed at her disposal for as long as she might require it. It was the prettiest bedroom she had ever seen, with a pale green carpet and curtains of oyster-pink moiré silk draped like a cascade at the tall windows, one of which opened outward onto a little balcony overlooking the gardens at the back of the house. There was a dressing table standing in a petticoat of oyster-pink satin and a mirror framed in beaten silver on the wall above the fireplace. There was a chair in which she could recline at full length with her feet on a padded footrest and a dainty writing table. And there were books on a little table beside her bed, which had a quilted headboard.

The first morning when she awakened it was to find a maid standing beside her with a daintily arranged breakfast tray. The maid placed the tray on a little table that extended across the bed and made the enjoyment of the piping hot coffee, served with cream that floated on top of it in rich, thick puffs, crisp rolls fresh out of the oven and golden pats of butter and cherry jam, an unalloyed pleasure.

At first Virginia imagined that she must have overslept and

was ready to apologize to the young woman whose name she already knew was Franzi, but the latter laugh and assured her in quite good English that Madame d'Auvergne *never* had breakfast outside her own room and all guests in the house were treated similarly.

She picked up a bed jacket from the foot of the bed and draped it around Virginia's shoulders over her simple pink nightdress, and Virginia felt almost embarrassed by so much attention.

"Madame is so crippled with the rheumatism that she does not find it easy to get about," the maid told her.

"Then perhaps there is something I could do for her?" Virginia suggested. She was suddenly inspired by an idea. "I could deal with her morning mail for her and answer her correspondence! And perhaps there are little errands I could perform for her."

Franzi laughed, showing excellent, strong white teeth. She was not much more than sixteen or seventeen, but so sturdily built and well developed that Virginia deduced she was a country girl, particularly as she had the most inviting roses in her cheeks.

"Madame will think the suggestion kind, but I doubt whether she will permit it to be carried out," she answered, thinking that the English young woman was not as excitingly beautiful as Mademoiselle Carla and her wardrobe could certainly not be compared with hers—Franzi had unpacked for Virginia the previous evening—but there was something about her that reminded Franzi of the first of the flowers when they appeared after the melting of the winter snows. Something delicate as the aconites and as simple as the marguerites that swept in a wave across the floor of the valley where her own home was.

And Madame d'Auvergne also laughed heartily when Virginia put forward to her her suggestions, declaring that in these days her mail presented few difficulties because she was such a bad correspondent. But she patted Virginia gratefully on her slim shoulder and told her what she could do.

"You can play chess with me every evening," she said. "And if you don't already know how to play, I will teach you. Léon is the only one who plays with me nowadays, but as he is always determined to win, and nearly always does, it is not so amusing."

So after dinner every evening, when no one came to visit them, Virginia played chess with her hostess in the salon that was hung with lilac mauve hangings and where the Empire furniture looked particularly right against a deeper mauve carpet. And in the mornings she sometimes went shopping for madame, exchanging her library books and matching ribbons and laces for her, for Madame d'Auvergne had a weakness for feminine frills and fripperies and loaded herself with them on every possible occasion. She also had a passion for jewelery such as rings, brooches, necklaces that flashed on her broad bosom, and earrings that drew attention to the exceeding delicacy of her ears. When guests came to dinner she usually appeared dripping with diamonds and finely graded pearls. Black velvet was her favorite evening wear, and it made her high-piled hair look particularly magnificent.

Among the people who dined with them during the first week of Virginia's stay at the villa was Mrs. Van Loon, whose house and garden Dr. Hanson had pointed out to her. Mary Van Loon was American, and attractive in a way that appealed to Virginia. Although she appeared very young and alive and brilliant under the sparkling light of chandeliers, in daylight she seemed rather faded and there was a weariness in her smile that Virginia found touching. It was a whimsical smile, too, and she had a strong sense of humor that made her exceedingly likable. Her husband was not there; he collected art treasures from all over the world and was often away from her for months at a time, which might have accounted for the disillusioned look on her face.

In coloring she was as fair as Carla Spengler, but there was nothing else of Carla about her.

Virginia knew that she would never forget that afternoon

when she had first arrived at the villa, and Carla had looked in on them unexpectedly to say goodbye before leaving for Italy. She had embraced Madame d'Auvergne with affection and turned and held out both her hands to Dr. Hanson, giving him a smile that was calculated to melt the bones of any man who admired her. Then she had turned to Virginia and studied her for a moment with upraised eyebrows, plainly trying to recall where she had seen her before.

"Oh, of course!" she exclaimed at last. "We have met before, haven't we? At the Milano! You bumped your head and Léon tried to help you."

"Miss Holt didn't bump her head," Dr. Hanson interjected with a slight smile. "It was bumped for her!"

"Oh, yes, of course! Those appalling young men! One of them must have spent too much time in the bar."

"I don't think so," Virginia said quite gently. "It was purely an accident."

The Spengler eyebrows were lifted again. "It's nice of you to look at it in that way, but personally I would have been furious," she declared. She looked at Léon Hanson. "Has Miss Holt become a patient of yours, then, Léon, as a result of that evening? And are you continuing to attend to the damage she received?"

"Not at all," he assured her, looking at Virginia whimsically. "Miss Holt is now more or less intact, but it is her sister who is a patient of mine. She is up at the clinic and Miss Holt was left stranded at the Milano. Aunt Héloise decided that it would please her immensely if Miss Holt would become her guest, and I brought her here barely a quarter of an hour ago. I think between us we have persuaded her that she is a welcome guest."

"Really?" But there was a cool note in Carla's sudden drawl. "Then you are fortunate, Miss Holt. This house is even more comfortable than the Milano."

"Yes, I realize that," Virginia answered a little uncomfortably.

"Nonsense!" Aunt Héloise exlaimed. "Once upon a time,

when I didn't have to bother about making the most of my income, as I do now, I *did* rather pride myself on being the sort of hostess my guests liked to stay with. But nowadays, what with the aftereffects of two wars and one thing and another, I just hope that they won't be induced to leave me too soon." She smiled very kindly at Virginia. "I am counting upon Miss Holt's being my guest for several weeks."

Carla turned away as if the subject had ceased to interest her, and she slid one of her slender white hands inside Dr. Hanson's arm.

"Léon, *chéri*, what are we going to do tonight to celebrate my departure? Something special because I will not see you again for weeks!"

"In that case a celebration seems uncalled for," he replied.

She regarded him with softened eyes for several seconds. "Nevertheless, we must do something!"

"Must we?" He looked down at her with a faintly caressing light in his own eyes, or so Virginia thought. "How do you expect me to survive during your absence?" he asked.

She smiled at him, a light like a tiny, flickering blue flame leaping up and down behind her long eyelashes.

"Darling," she told him, "I do not wish you to find it very easy to survive without me. It would upset me very much if I thought that absence would not make your heart yearn for me a little."

He obeyed an obvious impulse and very lightly touched her cheek. "But even so you will not be persuaded to change your plans?"

She shook her head very decidedly. "No, darling—not even for you!"

When they left, Dr. Hanson with his hand beneath Carla's elbow as he guided her out to her car, Virginia and her hostess stood side by side in the window and watched their departure. Madame d'Auvergne signed a little.

"They are a handsome pair," she remarked, "but—" She shook her impressive white head.

"Are they—engaged?" Virginia asked a little hesitantly.

"No. At least not officially, although everyone is expecting an announcement of their engagement at any time. They have known one another for years, ever since they were boy and girl together, and he has always adored her and protected her against every form of unpleasantness that came her way. She adores him, too, but—I don't know!" She sighed again.

"Is it her career that is coming between them?" Virginia suggested with the clear-sightedness of an onlooker.

"It could be that," Aunt Héloïse admitted. "And perhaps in time they will find a solution." Then she turned and looked at Virginia a little curiously. "My nephew was greatly concerned about you," she said. "He disliked the thought of your being alone at the Milano very much. He will be happier now that you are here."

"Will he?" Virginia murmured and wondered why the dark self-possessed surgeon, with all the demands of his profession and the preoccupations of a love affair that was not running with the maximum amount of smoothness, should spare any thought for her.

Two days later when she visited Lisa at the clinic she found her entertaining—or being entertained by, she was not quite sure which— a strange young man. He was seated in a negligent manner on the balcony rail, appeared very long-limbed and athletic, and had his right arm in a sling. He also had very blue eyes and light hair that curled a little.

Lisa looked up at Virginia with sparkling eyes. "This is Clive Maddison, Jinny," she said. "Mr. Maddison, this is my sister!"

"How do you do?" He disentangled himself with infinite grace from the balcony rail, moved forward and extended his good hand to Virginia. She was not altogether surprised when she felt her fingers all but reduced to pulp.

"Are you a patient here, too?" Virginia asked, regarding him curiously and then examining her fingers with a faintly rueful expression on her face.

"For only another couple of days," he told her; "and then

it's heigh-ho for the cruel hard world again for me!" He looked
as if he normally regarded the world as anything but a cruel,
hard place. He dragged forward a chair for her and then
resumed his former perch on the rail. "Your sister's balcony
and mine adjoin," he explained, "so I saw no reason why I
shouldn't pop in occasionally and visit her, provided she
raised no serious objection." He glanced for an instant at
Lisa's vivid and animated face. "I haven't made myself too
much of a nuisance, have I, Miss Holt?"

"On the contrary," she assured him, "you've had a tonic
effect on my spirits. It's a little lonely here sometimes—" she
looked almost apologetically at Virginia "—and one is
inclined to brood. But having a chat with another victim does
a lot to restore one's morale. Mr Maddison," she added for
her sister's information, "got himself very badly smashed up in
a skiing accident, and it's only after a good many weeks that
he's able to get about like this."

"Oh, I'm sorry," said Virginia, regarding him. "But you
look very fit again now."

"I'm more than fit," he answered, "in fact I'm an absolute sham.
But you know how it is with these hospital johnnies. They have
to be a hundred percent certain." In his turn he was regarding
Virginia, and he thought secretly that, considering the two
were sisters, they were extraordinarily unalike, but that in their
differing ways they were remarkably attractive. "In a couple of
days I'll be free of this splint on my arm and then there'll be no
excuse whatsoever for anyone to feel in the least sorry for me.
Not that a certain amount of sympathy sometimes isn't welcome." There was a faint, humorous sparkle in his eyes.

"And will you be staying on in Switzerland or are you going
home to England?"

"I don't quite know yet. I had thought of staying on for the
summer as a tennis pro, working for one of the hotels, but
whether I can wangle that sort of job after this accident
remains to be seen. In any case, I'll need a lot of overarm
practice before they'll be likely to take me on."

"I see," Virginia said, and then a nurse appeared wheeling a tea cart and he stood up prepared to take his departure.

"No cup for me, I see," he observed. "I'll leave you two to have a heart-to-heart talk."

"No, don't please," Lisa begged to Virginia's surprise, looking up at him with a sudden little rush of color to her cheeks. "I'm sure another cup can be brought if you'll only stay. And Jinny won't mind." She caught the eye of the attractive Swiss nurse, who seemed to be smiling with faint amusement under her stiffly starched cap. "Mr. Maddison can have tea on this balcony, can't he, nurse?"

"But, of course."

The matter was settled and another cup was brought, and the pretty nurse looked at Clive Maddison with a positive sparkle of amusement in her bright brown eyes. It was clear that she was not altogether surprised by his conquest.

He grinned up at her.

"Thank you, nurse! I won't forget," he told her.

But on her way back to Aunt Héloise's villa Virginia felt distinctly surprised, and she thought over the events of the afternoon with still mounting astonishment. Lisa, who had never been known to display the slightest interest in any man, to request one who was virtually a complete stranger to stay and have tea with her! It was almost unbelievable!

Even if he was an extremely attractive young man, with the gift of making himself charming and a fellow patient at the clinic...it was still extraordinary....

CHAPTER FIVE

As IT HAPPENED. Virginia was able to congratulate Clive Maddison on his resumption of a more or less normal life on the very morning of the day that he was released from the clinic. She was emerging from a shop where she had just purchased a length of *broderie anglaise* that she proposed to try her skill at making up into an afternoon dress for herself, and an adorable little fleecy bed jacket that she had at last found for Lisa, and both neat parcels were under her arm when she saw Clive standing and waiting for her on the sidewalk.

He had obviously watched her go into the shop. He was grinning amiably and looked very debonair in a gray flannel suit.

"Hello!" he said. "I hope you've left yourself a little money to spend on some other occasion?"

Virginia's apple-blossom color deepened, and her eyes sparkled. "I find shopping in Switzerland absolutely ruinous to my pocket," she confessed, "but I can't resist the lure of the shop windows." She gazed up at him with interest. "Are you a free man now or do you have to report for a checkup occasionally?"

"Oh, no, I'm quite free, and staying at the Milano as symbol of my freedom!"

"But isn't that rather expensive?"

"Dreadfully expensive, but I'm hoping it will lead to better things. The manager is getting to know me and in time I trust he will reward me with the position as coach that I so badly need, and which, if I catch him in a sufficiently expansive mood, he may hand out to me. When that much is achieved I shall find somewhere cheaper and mark time modestly until the season starts. And now I want you to do something for me."

He put his hand under her elbow and led her up to a flower shop. "Are you visiting your sister this afternoon?"

"Yes. I've got something to take to her."

"Good! Then you can take her something from me, too."

When they came out of the shop Virginia was carrying an enormous bouquet of exotic hothouse flowers over which her small white chin just managed to peep, and Clive was carrying her parcels and a ribbon-tied basket of luscious fruits. But although they were thus loaded he was not happy until he had purchased another large box of choicest Swiss chocolates, also secured with an enormous satin bow, and Virginia was horrified by the amount of money he had spent. She remonstrated with him as he led her to an open-air café where he ordered coffee for the two of them, but he merely looked at her with a lazy, amused smile in his eyes and shook his head.

"Never spoil a ship for a ha'porth of tar," he recommended. "Likewise, if you want to do a good deed, do it well! So long as you can manage them and don't mind presenting my compliments to your sister with these evidences of my earnest desire for her complete and speedy restoration to health?"

"Of course, I don't mind," she assured him. "But Lisa will be cross with you for being so extravagant."

"I don't think she will," he returned. The smile in his blue eyes faded and they grew rather more serious. "Your sister is rather a wonderful young woman, Miss Holt."

"Oh, Lisa's tremendously plucky," Virginia agreed at once.

"It isn't only her pluck I'm thinking of," he murmured, absentmindedly throwing away his half-smoked cigarette and lighting another. "It's everything about her.... She's very intense, I know, but then she's also very brilliant—a musical genius, I should say. It takes something more than pluck to be prepared to sacrifice all that one can sacrifice for the sake of a dream, a burning ambition."

Virginia nodded her head somberly.

"Yes," she said, "I know. But Lisa's like that. She never did believe in half measures."

"If—if this operation is not a success what do you think will happen to her?"

"I hardly dare to think," Virginia confessed in a husky whisper.

He looked at her keenly for a moment and then away.

"This fellow Hanson, who operates at the clinic—have you a great deal of confidence in him?"

Virginia stared down at the cream floating in great, rich puffs on the top of her cup of coffee, and she asked herself: Had she a great deal of confidence in Léon Hanson? The answer was that she had—for some reason she had tremendous confidence in him as a surgeon who could do great things for Lisa.

"Speaking from my own experience," Clive continued while she was silent, "and because I know that I owe such a lot to him myself, I really do think that he is the one man who can help your sister. But even so, she's not exactly like me—I was badly smashed up, but I'm tough and I suppose I could put up even with more than I did have to put up with. But Lisa—she's so fragile.... She doesn't look to me as if she could stand very much more. She's already had to go through quite a bit, and those eyes of hers—they're so shadow-haunted, so enormous! If she's going to be badly disappointed and this operation is not a success, wouldn't it be better—"

He broke off, grinding his cigarette into the ashtray.

"Wouldn't what be better?" Virginia asked gently.

"Wouldn't it be better to get Hanson to tell her that he can't perform miracles—that is, if he has any doubt at all, and you probably know whether he has—and try to talk her into, well, a different frame of mind about her future?"

Virginia shook her head.

"There is only one future for Lisa," she said with conviction.

Maddison gazed rather ruefully into her face, and to her surprise, he sighed suddenly, a curiously ragged little sigh.

"I was afraid you'd say that," he told her. He stared at the enormous bouquet of flowers that was resting on her lap. "And I'm afraid I'm inclined to agree with you...."

A large car was crawling slowly past along the lakeshore—a large, gleaming, black car—and as she glanced up and noticed it Virginia instantly recognized the man they had so recently been talking about sitting behind the wheel. There was a slight blockage of traffic just then and the car came to a halt. Dr. Hanson looked around and Virginia automatically lifted her hand and waved to him, but the Swiss surgeon did not even reply with a nod. He seemed to look through her and her companion. And then the stream of traffic moved evenly on and Virginia, with an unaccountable little pink flush in her cheeks, felt Clive's eyes studying her again.

"That was Hanson," he said—as if she could have had the slightest doubt! "He's a moody chap sometimes, but then I suppose his sort of job would make a man moody. It would me—seeing so much of the seamy side of life...."

"I don't think he noticed us," Virginia said.

"Don't you?" He smiled curiously, thinking, as he studied her wide white bow and her light brown hair that sparkled in the sunshine, her gentle gray eyes and her sensitive mouth, that, had he not fallen so badly for Lisa, her sister, he *must* have been attracted by Virginia! "Well, perhaps he didn't," he agreed.

BUT THAT NIGHT Virginia learned that both of them had made a mistake.

It was one of those rare nights that Aunt Héloise looked forward to, when her nephew accepted an invitation to dine with her, and she was careful to invite no other visitors. She adored having him to herself, and Virginia being a guest in the house—and a guest for whom she had already formed a very genuine attachment—it was almost as good as having him to herself.

He arrived early and Virginia was alone in the salon when he walked in. She gave him her rather shy but very friendly smile and he shook hands with her briefly. It was the first time he had shaken hands with her, she recollected, and somehow the touch of his warm, firm fingers left her with the curious sensation of having made contact with something strangely vital.

He walked into the wide window embrasure and stood looking out at the dreamy enchantment of the garden in the light of the setting sun, and as she joined him and they stood discussing the splendor of the evening and the perfection of the view, she thought that the expression of his face was grave and a little reserved. For one moment she wondered whether something was wrong with her sister.

Her heart gave an uneasy bound, and she asked anxiously, "I—I suppose everything is all right at the clinic...?"

"So far as I am aware there is nothing to give rise to any anxiety in your sister's condition, if that is what you mean," he replied coolly.

Virginia flushed uncontrollably. "I'm afraid she is rather on my mind," she admitted.

He said nothing and very shortly they were joined by his aunt. During dinner the conversation was on a variety of topics and Aunt Héloise made particular efforts to include Virginia, and ensure that she had no feeling of being left out. But Dr. Hanson did not deliberately address any remark to her. After dinner they sat listening to a symphony on the radio while Madame d'Auvergne did a little fine embroidery work, but when all at once she started to nod over her bright silks, her nephew very skillfully removed them from her lap, placed a cushion comfortably behind her head and left her to enjoy a nap in her favorite straight-backed armchair.

Then he looked across the room at Virginia.

"It's a fine night," he said rather curtly. "Would you care for a breath of air outside? And there's something I'd like to talk to you about, if you don't mind."

"Why, of course," she answered, feeling her heart start to race again. *Was* there something he felt he should no longer conceal from her, she wondered. And would it upset her very much when she learned about it?

Outside he placed his fingers very lightly under her elbow and guided her across the cool crispness of the lawn in the direction of a flight of steps that descended onto a terrace bounded by a stone balustrade, which overlooked the lake. It was such a beautiful night that Virginia felt her breath catch at the loveliness of it with its coldly glittering stars reflected like huge diamonds in the placid waters of the lake. Never before in her life had she experienced anything quite so soul-disturbing as this—the dreamy beauty of the garden hidden from her eyes by the velvet mantle of the night, and with a young moon rising above the tops of the great chestnut trees, whose candles were touched by the delicate, pearly opalescence. The same faint light lay across the terrace, crisscrossing it in silvery bars.

There was a decided chill in the air, but Dr. Hanson had advised her to fetch a wrap so she was not cold. She stood beside him at the stone balustrade, nestling her chin into the soft gray fur stole, and he stood with his hands thrust deep into the pockets of his dinner jacket, staring at the magic surface of the lake while together they listened to the musical murmur of the water breaking in tiny wavelets not many feet below them.

It's a wonderful night!" Virginia exclaimed suddenly, a thrill like a little tremor in her voice. "I don't think I've ever know such a wonderful night before!"

"Haven't you?" He looked down at her, considering her, and then up at the frozen aloofness of the snows lying like a protecting mantle over the mountain peaks. "So you and young Clive Maddison know one another already?" he remarked, his voice very cool and even.

Virginia looked up at him quickly.

"How—how do you know?" she asked with a certain amount of amazement.

"It's very simple," he replied. "I saw you together this morning. And moreover you seemed to be absorbed in a very deep conversation and you had an enormous bouquet on your lap. Is Clive 'saying it with flowers' so soon?"

Virginia's eyes widened almost incredulously and for a moment she could hardly reply.

"But—but I waved to you!" she said. "And as you didn't make any sign of having recognized me I didn't think you could have noticed us. Why didn't you let us see that you saw us?" she asked, gazing into his dark, shut-in, austere face with a look of wonderment in her eyes. "Clive and I were having coffee together. I—I first met him at the clinic."

"Yes, I gathered that that was where you met him." He produced his cigarette case and offered it to her, and as he lighted her cigarette she thought that he seemed to be studying her face intently. "I suppose it's natural, as he's a countryman of yours, that you should get together."

"I—why, I—" She didn't quite know what to say but she did recognize that there was something almost hostile in the tone of his speech, and those brilliant dark eyes of his were detached and critical. "You probably know more of him," she said, "than I do, as he's a patient of yours—or was—but at least he was very good for Lisa while he was at the clinic and I feel that he helped to cheer her up enormously by looking in and chatting to her and taking her mind off herself. He's quite an entertaining young man."

"A very entertaining young man—to impressionable young women like yourself and your sister!" He was leaning up against the stone balustrade and there was a cynical uplift to his eyebrows and a kind of cool, amused smile at the corners of his mouth. "But, all the same, I wouldn't accept all he tells you as gospel truth if I were you, and I wouldn't feel too sorry for him when he tells you his hard-luck story. He's been living in Switzerland now for quite a while, existing more or less on his charm and his wits, and although he comes from a very good English family I don't think they're particularly eager to have him back home again. In fact I don't think they're at all eager."

Virginia was regarding him with a quiet gleam in her eyes.

"But that has nothing to do with me, does it?" she asked. "Or Lisa? So far as we are concerned, his affairs are his own—and quite private!"

She thought that his sudden smile was touched with a hint of humor.

"Which means that they are nothing to do with me, also? Well, no doubt you are right, but I've just succeeded in patching him up after a very nasty accident, and in the course of time I may have to do some more patching if he persists in willfully risking life and limb as he has a habit of doing. He disdains the commonplace and in your country you would describe him as a keen sportsman, which means that he spends half his life climbing mountains, undertaking hazardous enterprises with the utmost zest and excelling at all outdoor sports. He will never settle down and a dull desk-and-office routine would kill him. Yet he is popular with everyone he meets, including me!"

"Yet you don't hesitate to—to imply things against him!" Virginia accused him, feeling a little incensed by the unreasonableness of his attitude.

"I say nothing against him that he wouldn't endorse himself—and I am only warning you! This morning I was surprised to observe that you are already so very friendly."

"Is having coffee with a man you have only met once before in your life a symptom of overwhelming friendliness?" Virginia inquired with a faint edge to her voice. "And, in any case, I think you might have acknowledged both of us, especially as I waved to you."

"I might have acknowledged both of you if you had not appeared to be so engrossed in your conversation."

"Our conversation did not concern ourselves—" And then

Virginia broke off, biting her lip. For the moment she was inclined to forget how much she was likely to owe to this man and how much assistance he had already given her in the matter of providing her with such exceedinly comfortable accommodation, which was costing her nothing at all and had already been the means of introducing her to new friends and acquaintances, while Lisa's mind was relieved of any anxiety concerning her. Virginia only thought suddenely that he was rather overbearing and arrogant. What she did while she was in Switzerland was really no business of his, and in view of the fact that he himself was practically engaged to be married and all his friends were awaiting an announcement of his wedding, even if Clive Maddison *had* bought flowers for her and had decided to pay her very marked attention, Léon Hanson could have no justifiable reason for objecting.

But despite her little spurt of indignation—largely because he had practically spoiled the whole of dinner for her by causing her to imagine that something had gone wrong with Lisa, as a result of his determined and, as she now realized, disapproving silence—she was about to tell him that the flowers purchased by Clive had been meant for Lisa when he interrupted her.

With a low note of humor in his voice and perhaps a faintly apologetic note, also, he said, "You musn't be angry with me because I feel it's my duty to keep a kind of watchful eye on you while you are here. Although you may not be so very young in years, you do strike me as being particularly youthful when it comes to looking after yourself in a manner that I could approve. I haven't forgotten, for instance, that you allow young savages to slam hotel doors in your face—"

Virginia's expression instantly softened and she laughed a little.

"That was because I wasn't very bright that night."

"Perhaps you weren't, and you certainly did look very small and alone at that table beside the palm."

He had placed his fingers under her elbow again and was

guiding her back across the lawn to the house. Virginia glanced up at him in a surprised fashion, meeting a faint twinkle in his eyes in the moonlight.

"But—but I didn't know you saw me!"

"Nevertheless I did! And now—" giving her arm a very gentle squeeze, "we will say nothing more about Maddison, save that I wish you to be aware that he has a reputation as a charmer and it would be as well to be on your guard, and arrive at a subject that I believe will be of even greater interest to you."

Virginia did not ask him what that subject was but he could feel the whole of her slight figure tense a little as they moved toward the veranda steps.

"It is, of course, your sister. I shall operate very soon now, I think. She has improved so much in a couple of weeks."

"Oh!" Virginia exclaimed, and he thought that she went rather white as he looked down at her.

"Don't worry." His voice was very quiet and she could feel his fingers on her arm increase their pressure so that for an instant they almost hurt her. "Don't look so concerned, my dear child! All will be well with her, I feel sure."

"Oh—oh, do you?"

They had come to a halt at the foot of the veranda steps and Virginia looked up at him rather helplessly. She was wearing her blue evening dress, and in the moonlight it seemed to have lost all its color, as had her small, heart-shaped face. Her gray eyes looked large and were filled with anxiety. He said even more gently, "I think you can safely leave it to me."

Virginia was suddenly so filled with gratitude that she wanted to return that pressure on her arm by catching at his sleeve and clinging to it. He had the sort of personality that, arrogant though it might be at times, gave out waves of comforting strength and renewed courage and was full of a kind of magnetism. From the very beginning she had been aware of his magnetism—that very evening when he had touched her hand before dinner she felt as if it was something alive and vital that had deliberately sought to claim her as a kind of victim..., And now...!

Now she was all at once so strongly affected by it that she actually wanted to postpone the moment when this standing together in close proximity would end and they would move on and enter the house; when his strength would leave her and the comforting confidence that he made her feel would desert her, too.

Oh, no, she thought suddenly in a kind of terror, as the realization of what was happening to her swept over her. *Not that—not that! Not if there is to be any peace or any sort of happiness in the future...!*

"You're cold?" he said suddenly, in a concerned tone as he felt her shiver, and he hurried her up the steps and into the house. Madame d'Auvergne's cheerful voice called to them from the great salon, where she was once more engaged at her embroidery work. She looked as if she had had a good nap, nevertheless, and her eyes were bright and observant.

"It was unpardonable of me to fall asleep," she apologized, "but at least you had the good sense to take Miss Holt into the garden, Léon. It was such a perfect evening, and I fear it is always a little stuffy in here, because when I admit the air I admit the drafts, also, and those I detest." She was studying her guest's somewhat revealing face and it seemed to her that the attractive gray eyes, which were normally addicted to quite ready smiles and had a happy, anticipatory gleam in them sometimes, had become blank and a little bewildered, unless it was purely her imagination. And the sharpness of the night air had driven all the color out of Virginia's cheeks and she seemed to huddle for warmth in her unpretentious gray squirrel stole.

"We will have some hot coffee," Aunt Héloise said, "and another time Léon must remember that it is perhaps a little early in the year for moonlight strolls."

She patted the striped satin-covered settee on which she was seated. Virginia accepted the invitation to take the place beside her and helped her unravel a skein of silk. Léon Hanson stood looking down at her a little thoughtfully.

Shortly afterward he left the room, and then Aunt Héloïse inquired, with her eyes on Virginia's face, "It was perhaps the little sister that my nephew discussed with you in the garden? Is all not well with her?"

Virginia seemed to come out of a kind of bemused trance. "Oh, no—oh, yes! He did discuss her, and he thinks that she has improved very much in the last two weeks."

"Then that is excellent news. And he will shortly decide to operate, is that it?"

"I think so—yes," Virginia answered.

Madame d'Auvergne gave her slim shoulder an affectionate pat with her beringed hand.

"In that case, my child, you will have nothing to worry about, for Léon is the one to be depended on. Your sister is in good hands; she could not be in better."

Virginia smiled rather wanly.

"I think you are quite right," she agreed.

"There is no doubt about it," Madame d'Auvergne said. "I am right!"

But as her shrewd old eyes continued to dwell on her young guest's face she found herself wondering a little. If it was not the little sister who was causing the faintly bewildered, rather distressed look on the fair, English face, what was it? She felt that she would like to know.

CHAPTER SIX

THE NEXT DAY Virginia, who received many invitations to local houses and events as a result of being a guest of Madame d'Auvergne, went to a tennis party at Mrs. Van Loon's.

Mary Van Loon was still, as she described herself, a grass widow, but she knew a great many young people in the district and her beautifully laid-out courts were lively with laughter and the sound of cheerful, untroubled voices. Clive Maddison was there, ignoring the advice he had received before he left the clinic and taking part in a strenuous set with a pretty Belgian girl as a partner. Later he partnered Virginia, but she was so hopelessly out of practice that she feared she had let him down and apologized profusely when they wandered off the court. He would not admit that their defeat had been anything to do with her, however, and muttered gloomily that he would have to put in "a heck of a lot of practice," as he phrased it, if the man who he hoped hire him that summer was not to turn him down.

Virginia glanced at him curiously as they strolled down a walk in the direction of the lake. He looked almost too handsome in his well-cut white flannels, and he was already deeply bronzed and his brown hair curled crisply. But with the remembrance of Dr. Hanson's expressed opinion of him the evening before very fresh in her mind, she found herself looking for the signs of weakness and instability that should have been lying either at the corners of his mouth, in the shape of his chin or in the gaze of his very blue eyes.

But to her it appeared that he had a very good chin— perhaps a trifle obstinate—and his mouth was pleasant and curved easily into a smile, and his eyes found no difficulty in meeting her direct gaze at any time.

He fetched her an iced drink and they sat side by side in a couple of deck chairs in a shady spot where the scent of the lilacs reached them and the almost painful shimmer of the smooth surface of the lake was visible through a gap in some foliage. She asked him, "Don't you feel that you would like to return to England?"

"Not particularly." He gave her a look that was rather whimsical all at once. "Why? Should I want to go back?"

"It all depends on how long you've been away."

"That's true," he agreed. He swished at the toe of his shoe with the end of his racket. "I've wandered a bit in the past couple of years, but I can't say I've ever felt tremendously homesick. At least not any more than a good many other people!" He grinned around at her, rather awkwardly, she thought. "Any special news of Lisa yet?"

She told him that Dr. Hanson was well satisfied with her and that he proposed to operate soon.

"How soon?" Maddison inquired and there was nothing but complete seriousness in his face now.

"Oh, fairly soon, I should think," Virginia answered.

"You'll let me know when—when it's to be, won't you?" he said with a curious diffidence in voice and look. "I—I'd naturally like to know."

"Of course," Virginia replied. "That is," she added, "if it's possible and I know in time."

He nodded his head understandingly.

"I'll have to order something rather special in the way of flowers and so forth, to gladden her eyes when she comes out of the anesthetic."

Virginia could not repress a shudder at the mention of that word "anesthetic," and he gripped her wrist comfortingly with his lean, brown hand.

"Don't let it upset you too much," he advised. "Remember that it's Hanson who is doing the job, and Hanson is the fair-haired boy at the clinic!"

Her hostess took Virginia's arm after tea and asked her whether she would like to see the house and be introduced to some of the treasures her husband had brought home from various parts of the world. There was, for instance, the wonderful jade Buddha in the dining room and the Satsuma bowls and vases displayed in the drawing room. There was also an absolutely flawless Chinese carpet in the drawing room and some very rare prints and jade ornaments. In Mary Van Loon's own bedroom there was an exquisite Venetian mirror on the wall above her dressing table, framed in beaten silver, and the wine-red, exquisitely fluted silk curtains of her half-tester bed were reputed to have once formed part of the trappings of Marie Antoinette's ornate couch.

One room had been so recently and beautifully decorated as a nursery that it somewhat surprised Virginia, for she had imagined that the Van Loons were childless.

Mary smiled at her surprise and explained, "I'm expecting my brother's children to arrive and stay with me soon—in fact I've more or less agreed to take charge of them for a while. Their mother died about six months ago, and as their father, like Edward, my husband, leads anything but a settled life, we thought it a good plan to offer them a more permanent sort of home until, perhaps, they acquire a stepmother or are sent to school or something of the sort."

"Oh, but that will be nice!" Virginia exclaimed, thinking that it really *would* be nice, for she was particularly devoted to children and had a naive belief that everyone else felt the same way as she did about them. "How soon will they arrive? And aren't you looking forward to having them?"

"Well, as a matter of fact," Mary Van Loon confessed, a somewhat subdued twinkle in her eyes, "I'm a little at a loss to know what to do with them when they do arrive. They're at the somewhat awkward ages of six and seven respectively, and I understand they're a very lively pair who've never been accustomed to very much discipline. My brother has more or less ruined the girl, and the boy takes after his mother and is nothing if not headstrong. They're at present in the charge of a well-meaning aunt who is scared to deny them anything, and I'm wondering what the impact is going to be on this household when they finally reach here straight from America."

"Oh, but young children are not really difficult to manage," Virginia assured her easily, with memories of her two young brothers—who had never at any time in their lives been exactly tractable—softened by distance in her mind. "Not if you're genuinely fond of them and you let them see that you are."

"As simple as all that, is it?" Mary inquired with a decided look of amusement on her face this time. "Well, perhaps you'd like to come and look after them for me as you seem to have a natural aptitude?"

Virginia was slightly taken aback by this suggestion but she decided that her hostess was joking.

"As a matter of fact, I'd love it," she confessed—and she meant it as she looked round the large, airy night nursery in which they were standing, with its pastel pink walls and its specially constructed furniture, its dainty satin eiderdowns on the twin beds and pictures of birds and flowers executed on the white woodwork. Adjoining it was an equally attractive day nursery, having a peerless view of the lake and all the cascade of blossoms that made up the fairy-tale garden of the Van Loons's house—and a bathroom that was more luxurious than anything she herself had ever used.

"Well, then, why not?" Mrs. Van Loon suggested.

Virginia stood gazing at her in amazement. Mrs. Van Loon was extraordinarily slim and graceful; she was wearing a heavy white silk dress that breathed expensiveness and everything about her—including her gold charm bracelet that was so loaded with charms that the weight of it must have been almost too much for her slender wrist—breathed expensiveness, also. By contrast with her, Virginia, in her homemade linen, which certainly became her, and her lack of any sort of ornamentation save her neat and unimaginative wristwatch, was almost painfully homely. Yet somehow Virginia did not think that it was the realization that she was the kind of girl who had to earn her own living that had prompted this sudden and quite surprising offer of employment.

Mary Van Loon's color came rather noticeably as if she was all at once a little appalled by her own impulsiveness.

"My dear," she said quickly, apologetically, "forgive me for shooting that one at you! Don't think I honestly imagine you want to be employed as a children's nanny—or whatever the appropriate term is! I know you told me that you were someone's secretary in London—a lawyer or someone equally dull and deadly, wasn't it? And although I can't imagine you spending more than half your life in a drab lawyer's office, I do realize that children would be a bit of a comedown. But it suddenly occured to me—if you *did* think of staying on out here...?"

"I can't think of anything I'd like better than to stay on out here," Virginia told her with slightly wistful truthfulness. "In fact it's been such a wonderful experience—all this beauty and color and the new friends I've made—everything about it— that it's not going to be at all easy to settle down when I get home again."

Mrs. Van Loon sank down on to the wide window ledge and produced her cigarette case from her handbag. She offered it to Virginia and when both their cigarettes were alight she regarded the other through a blue haze of smoke.

"Assuming that this operation your sister is to undergo is a success, she will, I suppose, resume her interrupted musical career?" As Virginia nodded, her hands clasped together fervently, Mrs. Van Loon frowned faintly. "But what about you and your future? Don't tell me you're going on working for a dry-as-dust lawyer all your days? Because that would be too ghastly! You're so very attractive, so very English, and I'm sure there are lots of things you could do if you thought about it. Léon Hanson might find you something in the clerical line out here, if you *want* something in the clerical line, and if you like Switzerland. . . . And the climate here is perfect from now until the autumn and in the winter there are the winter sports. You could at least have fun."

"Don't make it sound too tempting," Virginia said, smiling a little at the other's concern. "But I wouldn't dream of troubling Dr. Hanson. He has been so kind already, persuading his aunt to let me stay with her and making everything so easy for me."

"I don't think his aunt required very much persuasion," Mary returned. She went on regarding Virginia, "Have you met Carla Spengler?" she asked rather abruptly.

"Yes," Virginia replied. She added, "She's very beautiful, isn't she?"

Mrs. Van Loon made an almost imperceptible movement with her shoulders.

"She's somewhat spectacular," she said. She studied the tip of her cigarette. "Most people in this part of the world think that she and Léon will make a match of it one day, but somehow I have my doubts!" She smiled at Virginia. "And now I must go back to my guests, my dear. But don't forget, if you should suddenly decide that you'd like a change, Peter and Paula will be arriving at almost any moment now—well, within the next week or so, anyway."

WHEN SHE GOT BACK to the villa Aunt Héloise met Virginia in the hall and told her that her nephew had telephoned during the afternoon. Virginia, with her heart doing one of those crazy leaps to which it was addicted these days, felt the color receding from her face as she asked, with a catch of the breath, "Do you mean that he telephoned—me?"

Aunt Héloise shook her head at her chidingly and placed one of her plump hands on her shoulder.

"Now, my dear, foolish child, there is no need to look like that! Léon did ask for you, but I told him you were playing tennis and he insisted that the message could wait until you returned."

"What message?" Virginia demanded quickly.

"Only that he would call you again, perhaps this evening."

"Oh!" said Virginia as she sank down on to a spindly legged chair rather abruptly.

Madame d'Auvergne stood leaning on her ebony cane and regarding her with an extremely shrewd look in her eyes. Then she shook her head again, very slowly.

"It is not good," she said, "when the nerves play tricks and one is all on edge as you are at this moment. My nephew Léon would most certainly be highly disapproving! And therefore I shall insist that you go to bed early, whether he telephones or not, and we will have a little dinner served to us much earlier than usual in the small salon, and you will drink a very large tumbler of hot milk before you retire for the night, and that will induce sleep."

Her guest smiled at her wanly.

"You are kind," she told her.

Her hostess made a little clicking sound between her teeth and waved a hand to dissociate herself from any such thing.

But Dr. Hanson did not telephone that night, and but for the hot milk, reinforced with a couple of aspirin tablets, Virginia might have lain awake until the small hours wondering what it was he wanted to say to her. As it was she was all on edge at breakfast, which as usual was served to her in her room, and by lunchtime, as the telephone bell had not shrilled, Madame d'Auvergne had formed the resolution to take her with her on an afternoon's visit to an elderly English friend who had passed the winter in one of the little hotels that had not closed down and was much higher up the valley.

"You and she will have much in common," she said, "and it will do you good to talk to one of your own nationality. Quite apart from which I feel that I shall enjoy an outing myself."

In the face of this last observation Virginia felt that it would be ungracious in the extreme to try to avoid accompanying her hostess, and they set forth with Aunt Héloise smiling in secret to herself because she realized that Virginia was repressing her own wishes and merely being polite.

Still, but for the fact that her mind was more than half-occupied elsewhere, Virginia would have enjoyed that visit to the little hotel, standing knee-deep in spring flowers high up on a lush green ledge that overhung the valley and with all the wonder of the snows rising behind it. Miss Finch, the faded little elderly Englishwoman who could not stand the rigors of her own climate and yet was hungry for news of the well-remembered places—Bond Street and Piccadilly, the Green Park on a Sunday afternoon, Hampstead Heath where she used to exercise her dog—plied her with so many questions that she was forced to thrust her own affairs into the background of her mind for the time being, and Madame d'Auvergne sat complacently in her chair and consumed far more cream cakes than were good for her, as she well knew, while the other two chatted.

But when the typically English tea was over and it was getting on toward the dinner hour, Virginia began to grow anxious. Madame d'Auvergne looked as if she was fully prepared to remain and have dinner with her friend, and it was only because Pierre, her elderly chauffeur, disliked mountain roads after dark that she decided they really must leave. Virginia followed her thankfully out to the car.

When they returned to the villa there was still no message for Virginia, however, and it was not until after dinner that the summons came. Dr. Hanson's secretary spoke to her crisply, coolly, over the telephone. Dr. Hanson was sending his car to convey her to the clinic and he would see her when she reached there.

Virginia, with the telephone receiver shaking in her hand, asked in a voice that shook just as much, "Does this mean that there is something wrong with my sister?"

"No, nothing wrong. You will be able to see her as soon as she comes out of the anesthetic."

"The anesthetic? Oh...!"

"The car will arrive for you in about ten minutes."

Madame d'Auvergne came up silently behind Virginia,

took the receiver out of her hand and replaced it on its little ivory rest. She smiled at the shocked face of the girl.

"I was expecting you would hear something about this time," she said, "and in any case Léon knew perfectly well what I intended to do with you today. Had it been necessary he could have contacted you at any time."

"But—Lisa—" Virgnina's voice would not go on.

"Lisa will prefer that it will be her sister there beside her bed when she opens her eyes and therefore if you wish to make any changes to your dress I would recommend you to hurry. Would you like me to come with you, my dear?"

But Virginia shook her head.

"No, thank you. I'll be all right."

"I'm quite sure that you will." Aunt Héloise gave her shoulder a little reassuring pat.

In the car, when it arrived, Virginia lay back against the silver gray upholstery and felt as if she were a balloon from which someone had unexpectedly released the air. She had no real feelings—she was not even capable of thought. Her hands were clammy inside the thin nylon gloves she had snatched hastily out of her dressing-table drawer and her feet were cold as if she had been badly shocked. And in a way she had. For although Dr. Hanson had no doubt decided that to spare her the long-drawn-out ordeal of knowing that Lisa was to be operated on that day was the sensible thing, she knew that she herself would have much preferred it otherwise.

All that she could think of now was that something could have happened to Lisa and she would not have been on hand to see her before it was too late. Lisa had had to face her ordeal without any member of her family near her, and to Virginia that seemed worse than heartless. It was typical of the calm levelheadedness of Léon Hanson, but she was not prepared to admit he was right. She was even, as his expensive car whirled her almost silently to the clinic, prepared to nurse a dull feeling of resentment against him because he had taken so much upon himself and had not even consulted her over such an important matter.

But when she reached the clinic her mind had awakened to one urgency only and that was to see Lisa. The cool white walls of the beautifully planned building received her, and the matron herself came to have a few words with her in the little room to which she was taken.

"Miss Holt is not yet sufficiently conscious for you to see her," she was told, "but I'm sure you would like a cup of tea while you are waiting, wouldn't you? Dr. Hanson will be in to see you in a few minutes."

"Then he is still here?" Virginia said. Her lips were shaking uncontrollably and she put up her handkerchief to hide them.

The matron's smile was completely understanding and sympathetic.

"Yes, he is still here and I think I can tell you quite truthfully that he is very well satisfied with the results of the operation so far."

"Then—then Lisa is not in any danger?" she asked.

The matron's little shake of the head was most reassuring.

"She is as comfortable as can be expected at the moment."

When she had left the room Virginia drank the tea that was brought to her and studied the pictures on the walls, and the bowl of flowers on the table. Outside the window with its little balcony there was that wonderful view that could never fail to enchant her, and with the last of the light lingering on the rose-flushed mountain peaks and the lake a shadowy purple pierced by the magic of the first stars that were hanging like lamps in the great, dusky void above, there was something soothing and reassuring about it. Virginia went to stand by the window and let the loveliness of it all seep into her soul. She thought, because her mind was a kind of incoherent whirlpool, if anything *had* happened to Lisa and she had to stand like this beside the window waiting for someone to come to her, how would she have felt about the view?

Would it have saddened her inexpressibly or would it simply not have been there ...?

The door opened without any sound whatsoever and Dr. Hanson stood regarding her in his white coat.

Virginia had never seen him before in a white coat, only in his well-cut suits and evening dress, and her first thought was that he looked like another person somehow. He seemed remote and like a complete stranger, and even his eyes were detached. He came quietly into the room and shut the door firmly and then turned to her.

"Good evening, Miss Holt. I expect they'll allow you to see your sister before very long."

Virginia's gray eyes were large and accusing.

"Why didn't you let me know it was to take place today?" she inquired with a quite noticeable quiver in her voice.

He glanced at the tea things on the table and even examined the teapot to make sure that she had consumed its contents.

"If you would like any coffee or even more tea you have only to ring, you know," he told her in a rather abstracted voice.

"I don't want any coffee or any more tea," Virginia almost flung at him, "but I do want to know why you operated on Lisa without letting me know that you intended to do so? It wasn't fair!"

"Wasn't it?" For a moment she might have been back in the garden of Madame d'Auvergne's villa on the shore of the lake, with the night wind stirring the trees and his hand under her elbow guiding her across the lawn, for there was no longer any detachment in his voice, and his eyes looked down into her own with a softened expression that brought her close to him. "Wasn't it?" he repeated very gently. "But I thought it the wisest thing to do, and it seemed so senseless to keep you in a state of uncertainty and anxiety for hours on end. You've got rather a vivid type of imagination, and it's not very kind to you on occasions such as this."

That was so true that Virginia could not dispute it, but there was still Lisa who had been deprived of the consolation of her presence—if it could possibly have been any consolation to her—here in the clinic while her whole future existence was being decided for her. And Lisa was the one who really counted!

"Perhaps you'll feel a little less indignant if I tell you that it was your sister's idea as well," Léon Hanson told her, still gazing at her with that faintly indulgent and very sympathetic gleam in his deep dark eyes. "In fact, she was quite insistent about it and as I agreed with her you were not told. I hope you're not going to feel that you've been hardly used?"

"Oh, of course not." But a film of emotion rising behind her eyes made Virgina blink her eyelids rapidly. "That's so like Lisa. She's tremendously plucky."

"She is," he agreed. He watched her maltreating her gloves with her restless fingers and suddenly put out his hands and took both of hers, crushing them rather hard. "You'll feel better when you've seen her. But she won't be able to say much to you tonight and you won't be allowed to remain with her for more than a few minutes."

"But she is going to be all right?" she asked, meeting his direct look.

"I'm fairly certain she's going to be quite all right!"

Virginia blinked more rapidly, for a tear was actually beginning to trickle down one side of her nose. And it was to him they owed it! To him Lisa would owe everything!

She gulped suddenly and turned away, blowing her nose heartily.

He put his finger on the bell push.

"I really think you could do with some more tea!"

Lisa looked so unlike Lisa when Virginia bent over her in the faintly lit room that she felt almost as if she was encouraging a stranger.

"You're going to be all right, darling! Quite all right!"

Lisa's enormous dark eyes reflected a glimmering of understanding and then smiled a little.

"Of course," she whispered. Her pale lips seemed to be framing other words, and Virginia bent closer until she felt her sister's faint breath on her cheek. "Tell Clive—do you mind—"

Virginia answered at once, "Of course not, darling. I'll let him know immediately."

"Good for you, Jinny!" Lisa whispered, smiled more naturally at her, and then, like a weary child, let her eyelids fall and seemed to go off into a kind of tranquil doze.

Virginia tiptoed from the room and found Dr. Hanson waiting for her on the other side of the door.

"I'll take you home," he said. "You've had rather an exhausting evening."

"Do you think I could use the telephone first?" Virginia inquired.

"Of course," he answered, "if it's important. But won't it wait until the morning?"

"Well, no," Virginia told him. "You see, I want to call Clive Maddison and let him know about Lisa—"

But as soon as she had mentioned Clive's name she knew that it had been a mistake. Léon's dark eyes seemed to give a cold flash and the jut of his chin became noticeable. He said with a note like polite ice in his voice:

"Then he can certainly wait until the morning! And now, if you're ready, we'll go."

Virginia realized that there would be little point in pursuing the matter, and for one thing it was rather late to put through a call at his hotel to a man about whom she actually knew very little. There would be time enough in the morning. And she had no desire to antagonize Dr. Hanson tonight, for, as she kept on saying to herself, but for him—

But for him Lisa would not now be lying tranquilly in her white hospital cot with a look of the utmost serenity on her face and her whole future, perhaps, given back to her!

Her whole future . . .!

Virginia was glad of the darkness of the interior of the car, which Dr. Hanson's chauffeur drove tonight, for every time she thought about Lisa the lump rose in her throat and she knew that the absurd tears would persist in welling over her eyelids. There were so many questions she wanted to ask Dr. Hanson—questions about Lisa's convalescence and how long it would be before she would be able to use her hands and whether the exercises he would prescribe would have to be carried out over a long period—but he was not an easy man to approach and tonight he seemed very silent as he lay back in his corner of the car. Virginia stole cautious glances at him every now and again and saw that he was staring at the softly gleaming roof lamp.

A small sigh escaped her suddenly before she could prevent it, and it was a tired and rather ragged sigh.

He put out his hand and covered both of hers that were lying limply clasped in her lap.

"You're tired?" he said quickly. "You'll be glad to get to bed. And tomorrow you'll be able to see your sister again."

"Dr. Hanson—" she was fumbling for words "—Dr. Hanson, if Lisa's going to be all right again it will be all due to you!"

"Well, what of it?" he asked, a queer little smile at the corners of his mouth as he regarded her intently through the gloom.

"What of it?" She caught her breath again. "Oh, don't you realize...!" She broke off, tightening the clasp of her hands while his still rested over them as if he had forgotten to remove it. "Dr. Hanson," she said rather breathlessly, "whatever your fee for this operation you performed tonight on Lisa and all your care of her, we shall always be in your debt—*nothing* can really repay you!"

Her eyes were enormous in her pale face and he could feel the tenseness of her fingers, the emotion that was coursing through her.

He said gently, "I don't think we'll discuss fees tonight, do you? If we ever discuss them! Instead I would like you to relax a little and forget everything for the time being." He suddenly slipped his hand behind her and pulled her up against him, forcing her head down into the hollow of his shoulder. "Now, shut your eyes and let your mind become a peaceful blank! Or, if you must think, think only of pleasant things...."

Virginia could actually hear the beating of his heart just under her ear and it seemed to her to be a remarkably strong and steady beat compared to the wild panic of her own suddenly racing pulses. He had ordered her to think calmly—if she must think at all—but every quivering instinct she possessed was responding to this unexpected close contact with him and a kind of shivering excitement took possession of her so that all thoughts of Lisa were driven out of her mind.

"I have been making plans," he told her, "over the past few days, and if all is well with your sister by the weekend—as I feel certain it will be—then you and I will steal away and have a day to ourselves somewhere. Would you like that? A day in the mountains if the weather is fine, and I will show you something that you will never see in England. I will give you a little picture of my country to carry away with you—a mental picture that you can look at and examine in later days, and that will serve to remind you of your visit here. What do you say?"

"I—I would love it," she answered, trying to still that wild clamor of her pulses and longing to ask him what Carla Spengler would think of their spending a day in the mountains together. Although had he not made it clear that it was to be merely an interlude—something she could look back upon in later days? If she were wise she would refuse. But she hadn't the strength of mind to refuse. "I would love it," she repeated, inhaling the faint perfume of cigarette smoke and shaving cream that clung about him.

"Good!" he exclaimed softly. "Then you will keep Sunday free for me and if anyone else—Monsieur Maddison, shall we say—should ask you to devote the day to him you will be ready with the polite refusal? Is that understood?"

"Of course," she murmured, and longed to turn her face right into his neck and just lie there peacefully with her eyes shut, with the knowledge that a drive of several hours was ahead of them instead of merely a few minutes longer. And those minutes passed.

When they drew up outside Madame d'Auvergne's villa he helped her to alight and then insisted on escorting her through the garden and up the steps to the closed-in veranda. Franzi, who had been sitting up for Virginia, opened the door for her and then was somewhat curtly dismissed by the doctor who ordered her to take hot milk to Virginia's room and to make herself useful to her if necessary.

But Virginia insisted that she did not really require hot milk and that Franzi must go to bed at once. She was full of apologies for having kept her up so late.

"Do not countermand my orders," Léon Hanson said, looking down queerly into Virginia's wide gray eyes. "Not only will Franzi take the milk to your room but you will drink it!" Franzi disappeared from the hall and he lifted Virginia's hand and, after a moment's hesitation, carried it up to his lips. "Good night, my little one!"

Virginia's heart stopped beating for a moment.

"Good night," she whispered, "and—and thank you for—everything ...!"

CHAPTER SEVEN

To Virginia's relief it was not much more than a matter of days before Lisa was sitting up in bed and holding court in her room and by the end of the week she was allowed to sit on her veranda.

Her hand was still in bandages but she looked a very different Lisa already. There was a bright gleam in her eyes and a touch of color in her cheeks, and her outlook was so completely optimistic that Virginia could only keep her fingers crossed for her and trust most fervently that nothing would at this stage go wrong.

Not that Lisa talked so much about her future. She seemed almost completely content in the present, especially when Clive Maddison was sitting in the chair beside her and entertaining her with his cheerful conversation. He had already caused the nurses to start teasing him because he was so often at the clinic—apparently he had fallen in love with it, they said—and he never made his appearance in Lisa's room without bringing her quantities of flowers and chocolates and anything else he thought she would like. When she protested because she knew he had to earn his own living he informed her debonairly that money was intended to be spent and once parted with it could never be spent again. And what better cause could he expend his on than the cause of a future concert pianist?

Virginia watched them when they were together, and she happened to be visiting her sister at the same time as Clive—and that was very nearly every afternoon!

There could be no doubt about it—and this astonished her

more than anything in life had astonished her before—Lisa was almost violently attracted to her young fellow countryman. Only he could bring that slightly feverish sparkle to her great dark eyes and only his departure could dim the sparkle, like someone abruptly extinguishing the wick of a lamp.

Lisa was so transparent where her feelings were concerned that Virginia sometimes felt vaguely uncomfortable and apprehensive. Before she had had to listen to Lisa bewailing the almost brutal way in which all her future hopes had been blighted and her outlook on life rendered overcast, but now, instead of chattering about the moment when the bandages could be removed from her hand and the exercises to render her fingers supple again could begin, she chattered to Virginia about Clive's hopes of getting the job of tennis coach his heart was set on and about the various misfortunes and accidents that had prevented him from holding down any particularly good job for long.

She was eager to defend him because he was something of a rolling stone—and even she was aware that a rolling stone gathered very little moss. Virginia ventured to remind her of that one day, but Lisa instantly replied that in Clive's case it wasn't because he *wished* to be unconventional and drift from place to place, apparently shirking responsibilities—already he knew most of the capitals of Europe—save, of course, those tucked firmly away behind the Iron Curtain—and had visited Australia and New Zealand and even tried looking for a job in Canada—but because fate was inexorable and would not allow him to vegetate for long in one place.

"But one day he'll settle down," Lisa said optimistically. "I know he will."

Virginia was not so optimistic. She wondered sometimes what her parents would say if they knew about this sudden change of heart of Lisa's. It would no doubt perplex them extremely because music, which had been her whole world, was no longer even a part of her world.

The truth was that Lisa hardly ever spoke about music these days.

As for Clive himself it would have been difficult to form any opinion as to what his real feelings were for Lisa. He was charming to her and most attentive, but then he had been charming and attentive to quite a few women in his life if all that she had heard about him was true. He went out of his way to be specially nice to Virginia; it was true he had not so far loaded her with gifts, but he made a habit of waylaying her when she was shopping in the mornings and persuading her to have coffee with him at the little open-air café on the shore of the lake. And he had an open invitation to so many houses in the district that she was almost certain to meet him when she went visiting with Madame d'Auvergne. Hostesses had formed a habit of pairing them together because they seemed to know one another so well and this was sometimes a little embarrassing for Virginia.

It was embarrassing, for instance, when Léon Hanson was also a guest, as he was at one dinner party, and the fact that he avoided her very noticeably all evening and left without saying goodbye to her—it was true that his hostess explained that he had been called away—made her almost deathly miserable throughout the whole of the next day.

But the day following was the day on which she was to go for the trip into the mountains with him and she looked forward to it with so much bottled-up pleasure at the thought that she felt she simply could not have endured it if anything had happened to interfere with their arrangement.

She had told Lisa about the expedition the day before and Lisa had at first looked mildly astonished. Then a gleam of interest had entered her eyes as she studied her sister.

There was something about Virginia's expression just then that gave away a good deal, and Lisa said gently, "Oh, I do hope you have a lovely day! Wear your primrose linen and that fleecy white bolero thing Aunt Kay knitted for you. You look so nice in it. And put a ribbon in your hair—a ribbon in your hair suits you."

"I shall look like an Easter egg all dolled up for the occasion with a ribbon in my hair," Virginia protested.

"Nonsense!" Lisa exclaimed. "You'll look Virginia-ish, and Dr. Hanson will like you that way."

"He probably won't even notice what I wear. He's merely taking me off his aunt's hands for a day."

"Do you honestly think so?" Lisa looked at her keenly. "Is that what you really think, Jinny?"

"What else would I think?" Virginia was conscious nevertheless of the absurd color welling up over her face and neck. "Madame d'Auvergne has almost worn herself out devising what she calls distracting little entertainments for me. They both have a kind of idea that unless I'm unceasingly occupied I'm inclined to dwell upon you and worry about you—which I can assure you I don't do now that you're looking so blooming!"

Lisa suddenly looked thoughtful. She was wearing the pretty pink bed jacket Virginia had bought for her and was toying with an end of one of the satin ribbons that secured it at the neck.

"Did you know, Jinny, that Dr. Hanson suggested to me that as soon as I am able to leave here—in about another week or possibly less—he would like me to become a guest of his aunt while he gets someone to start exercises on my fingers?"

Virginia looked almost startled. "No, I didn't," she admitted.

"I wondered whether he had mentioned it to you." Lisa stared down at the ribbon and then at the highly professional-looking bandages on her right hand, which made it look twice its size. "Of course I told him that we couldn't both take advantage of Madame d'Auvergne's kindness and I meant it. We *couldn't* expect her to act hostess to us both, could we? You agree with me, don't you, Jinny?"

"Why, I—why, yes." But Virginia still looked as if she had received something in the nature of a mild shock. "Of course I agree. And that means that one of us must go home and that one certainly won't be you!"

"Well, darling, I'm afraid it will have to be you, but—" Lisa paused "—what about Dr. Hanson?" she asked rather abruptly.

"Dr. Hanson?" Virginia stared at her. "What has Dr. Hanson got to do with my going home?"

Lisa's expression softened and her eyes grew faintly concerned.

"Don't pretend, idiot," she said softly. "You like him, don't you? But if he likes you your going home to England won't make a scrap of difference."

"For goodness' sake, Liz," Virginia exclaimed, jerking up her head like a young, startled pony, "stop talking such a lot of nonsense! Dr. Hanson is as good as engaged to Carla Spengler and their friends are merely awaiting an announcement that the wedding day has been fixed! How can you start thinking such crazy thoughts?"

"I wouldn't be prepared to swear they're crazy," Lisa said, faintly amused by the look—of horror almost—on her sister's face. "And what has this Carla Spengler got that you haven't got—except a voice."

"She's absolutely beautiful," Virginia told her.

"Well, as you know, I've never considered you exactly plain."

"We're not even in the same class," Virginia muttered rather wistfully. And then she started to gather together her gloves and handbag. "I must go now, and I hope during your moments of quiet reflection you'll grow a little more rational!"

"I might," Lisa admitted, "but, on the other hand, I might not!" She looked rather sorrowfully at her sister. "I'm honestly sorry, darling, to cut your little holiday short—and I believe you've enjoyed it even though you've had me on your mind—but unless you can think of some way of staying, apart from turning Madame d'Auvergne's villa into a kind of unofficial hotel—"

"There isn't any way," Virginia said. And then suddenly she

remembered Mary Van Loon. There *was* a way...but why go on staying out here in Switzerland when there was no special reason why she should stay? All good things came to an end sometime! But, all the same, Mary had offered her a job and Mary did need help. And she was very fond of children. She was not altogether looking forward to taking up secretarial duties again, especially in a stuffy office tucked away in one of the least salubrious thoroughfares of London.

She would give the matter of Mrs. Van Loon thought....

And then she hurried away before Lisa could guess that an idea had entered her mind. Lisa might wish to discuss it with her and try to influence her decision....

CHAPTER EIGHT

BUT SHE DECIDED to think of nothing that was in the very slightest degree unpleasant, when Sunday morning dawned in a lilac haze that promised early summer heat as the day advanced, and the telephone had not rung to prepare her for a postponement of the outing, or perhaps its cancellation altogether. Virginia, up as soon as she had swallowed her morning coffee and rolls, splashed happily in her bath and then dressed with more care than she had ever expended on her dressing in her life.

Lisa had been right about the primrose linen dress. It became her better, possibly, than anything else in her wardrobe and somehow the ribbon looked right, as well. When she went into Madame d'Auvergne's bedroom to say goodbye to her, her hostess raised herself on her small mountain of pillows and looked at her with approving eyes.

"You look immensely chic, my child," she said, "and you also look quite delightful! More and more you remind me of myself when I was young!"

Virginia accepted the compliment gratefully, for although Aunt Héloise, in her enormous bed with the curly bedposts, the cupids and the garlands of flowers and fruit entwining them and the mulberry satin curtains and eiderdown, looked large and a trifle florid in her mauve lace bed jacket, she still had enough in the way of good looks, and especially her wonderful silvery hair, to make this a compliment worthy of acceptance.

"You go now to enjoy yourself, and I hope you will teach my nephew to relax a little, also." When her nephew arrived he went in to bid her good-morning and kissed the lightly powdered cheek she turned to him. "Take care of this child, Léon, and return her to me at a reasonable hour," she instructed him.

He looked at her with faintly twinkling eyes.

"You are not afraid to trust her to me?"

Madame d'Auvergne's eyes twinkled in return.

"Not at all. She will be, I fear, almost too safe with you!"

When they were outside and seated in his big black car, Virginia could feel the color hot in her cheeks, and she knew that Léon Hanson was looking and feeling a little amused. He cast her a sideways glance before he slipped in his clutch and there was something a trifle provocative in his voice when he remarked, "That old aunt of mine has a somewhat perverted idea of the fitness of things at times! And I'm afraid she has a rather puckish idea of humor as well."

"I think she's delightful," Virginia answered truthfully, but still not daring to look directly at him, "and I've grown very fond of her these last few weeks."

"Have you? That's good!" He piloted the car away from the curb. "And you haven't any qualms yourself about spending a whole day in my company, not knowing where I propose to take you or what sort of plans I've formed for your entertainment?"

Virginia sat clutching her little white bag in her lap and staring down at the open toes of her sandals.

"No, I haven't any qualms," she admitted.

"That's splendid," he told her softly and rewarded her with a brilliant smile. "Now let's do what I said and forget everything and have a thoroughly good time."

So far as Virginia was concerned the good time was memorable and there were to be days ahead in her future when she looked back upon this Sunday as a day of purest magic, which glowed as no other Sunday in her life had ever glowed.

True, they were not doing the things one normally did on a Sunday, such as going to church. But as Dr. Hanson spent most of his weekdays serving other people she felt strongly that he had a right to shed care and responsibility and be someone other than the correct Dr. Hanson who belonged strictly to his consulting rooms and the clinic, one day of the week at least. And Sunday was not by any manner of means a usual day of recreation for him. This was one snatched for some whim of his own out of the blue.

To begin with he drove superbly, and once on a clear road that led—or seemed to lead—right into the very heart of the mountains, he went at considerable speed, which Virginia thoroughly enjoyed. It caused the warm wind to sing past her ears and the blue and gold loveliness of the morning was like a dream unfolding before her eyes. At her side Léon Hanson looked much younger, she thought, in flannels and a blazer, and for once she did not feel any awe of him and was no longer afraid to be entirely natural in his presence.

She was able to feel relaxed and almost light-headedly happy. He was quick to sense that she was no longer in any degree on the defensive with him and he responded in a way that increased her happiness.

If she had been afraid that he would remember Clive Maddison and tax her about him she need not have done so. He had forgotten everything unpleasant, as she had, and the day therefore was unspoiled.

They had lunch at a little hotel high up in the mountains where the waiters quite obviously knew Dr. Hanson well and were most deferential. Their table was placed on a balcony overlooking a valley where the flowers of high summer were rapidly replacing the flowers of late spring. Again it was like being in a box at the theater and looking down on a really spectacular drop scene, where toy cattle grazed knee-deep in perfumed sweetness and the wooden walls of a farmhouse and the spire of a church rose into the unbelievably clear atmosphere.

Virginia thought, *This must be one of the mental pictures I am to look at when I return to England!*

And how often, *how often* would she feel the imperative urge to look at it?

Léon Hanson noticed that a faint shadow spread over her face as she gazed downward into the valley, and he pushed her glass of wine nearer to her.

"This is not a day on which you will be permitted to look wistful," he observed. "This is a day on which you banish care!"

Virginia met his eyes with their softly black and yet strangely gleaming expression, and her heart did a somersault.

"I was merely thinking that this is one of the pictures you promised me I would take home with me when I go," she said, thinking that if she stared into his eyes long enough he would have the power to mesmerize her.

"There will be others," he replied, smiling at her indulgently while the waiter poured their coffee. "There will probably be quite a lot of others!"

Before they left the hotel he collected a hamper containing all the essential items for a picnic tea and then they drove on again through the drowsy warmth of the afternoon until at last they reached the welcome shade of a little pine wood. The air was saturated with the aromatic scent of the pine needles. A tiny cascade of crystal clear water came bounding down from the heights above them and disappeared into a silvery river below and a rustic bridge overhung the river. There was green twilight beneath the trees and Virginia knew at once that here was another picture she would never forget.

"I think we'll stop here," he said, "and until you feel the urge to sample the contents of that picnic basket you can talk to me about all the things you do when you are at home in England. I'd like to hear something about the kind of life you lead and then I can judge whether it is wildly exciting or not." His eyes were laughing at her as he flung a coat down onto the pine needles and she dropped onto it with natural grace. "Now, let me hear the worst!"

"There is so little to tell," she replied, watching him as he stretched himself out full-length and stared upward through the thickness of the branches to the little patch of blue sky just visible above their heads.

"That I decline to believe," he answered, and feeling automatically for his cigarette case, passed it to her. As she selected a cigarette he sat up to hold his lighter to it.

"Now tell me the truth," he ordered. "What do you do when you are at home?"

"Nothing in the least exciting."

He held the lighter to his own citarette and watched her above the flame.

"Well, what are the unexciting things you do?"

She gave him a little word picture of their way of life on Cromwell Road—and how far away that seemed to her now, almost as if it were not actually real—making her daily pilgrimage to her office sound a little monotonous, to say the least, and the occasional tennis club dance and meeting of the Ramblers' Society, uninspired affairs which made him crinkle his dark brows. He regarded her under his thick eyelashes and noticed how well the yellow linen became her, how the ribbon looped through her curls was not more golden than some of the lights in her hair, and what a peaches-and-cream loveliness glowed in her complexion. And she had a demure mouth that fascinated him because there was always something wistful about it, even when she smiled.

"And there are no ardent admirers who wish to remove you from this dull existence and make it perhaps a little more colorful?"

Virginia answered truthfully that there were none that she knew of, whom she favored, at least.

"But there are those whom you do not favor but who are inclined to pester you?"

"I have never been pestered by an admirer in my life," Virginia admitted and thought, even as she made the admission, how very dull and insignificant she was compared with, for instance, such a creature of glamour as Carla Spengler. And one day he would almost certainly marry Carla!

"Then your countrymen must be sadly lacking in initiative," the doctor observed, leaning on his elbow and studying her thoughtfully while the smoke from his cigarette curled upward toward the pine tops.

"Do you think so?" She gave him a little, quick, shy smile.

"I certainly think so!"

His eyes were on the softly formed lips, pink as a carnation.

"I am going to ask you for a particular favor before we leave this pine wood, but in the meantime I wish to learn more about you. When you look back upon your stay here in Switzerland will it be with any pleasure or do you think that you will forget us all quickly?"

"I shall certainly not forget any of you quickly—" her breath caught in her throat and her pulses fluttered like a frightened bird's. All this was rather painful; he was making it so increasingly clear that she was merely someone who intrigued him a little and whose departure he could bear to think of, and think of with equanimity "—and my memories of Switzerland will be amongst the happiest I am ever likely to have to look back upon."

"That, at least, is good to hear!" He crushed out his half-smoked cigarette and absentmindedly lighted another. "My aunt is contemplating extending her hospitality to your sister when—as I think very likely—she leaves the clinic in a few more days. I wish to have her under my eye for a time while the exercises I have prescribed for her fingers are begun, and that will enable you two to be together for a while and enjoy a little holiday that may be very pleasant."

"It would be very pleasant if I could stay, but I have already greatly abused your aunt's kindness. She has given me a wonderful time and I can never thank her enough, but when Lisa leaves the clinic I must go home."

"Must you?" There was absolutely no change in his tone. "But surely there is not really a 'must' about it? My aunt would fill her house with young people if sufficient young people could be found who suited her taste."

"Your aunt is wonderful, but there is such a thing as out-staying one's welcome."

"I really don't think I can agree with that," he said as if he was examining the idea.

Virginia looked away from him and her fingers sank deep into the pine needles so that they pricked into her skin. All at once she decided to tell him. "Mrs. Van Loon did offer me a—a job looking after her small niece and nephew when they arrive from America, but I haven't yet made up my mind whether to accept it or not."

"Oh! Indeed?" He sat up as if this was of considerable interest. "Of course, I remember Mary is having her brother's children to stay with her, and the last time we met she was a little at a loss to know what to do with them." He studied her with a bright, appraising look in his eyes. "Are you fond of children?"

"Very."

"Then that solves the problem, doesn't it? If your pride won't allow you to continue to stay with my aunt, a job with Mary Van Loon is the very thing that is needed! You're almost certain to be happy with the Van Loons—although Edward is away so much you'll find that he's charming when he's at home. And I'm sure your sister would like you to stay. Besides, it seems a pity that you should go before you've seen these valleys thick with snow. You must learn to ski."

He was taking it for granted that she was going to accept this position as nursery governess or whatever it was—and for a moment the loveliness of the afternoon was dimmed by the depressing thought that to him it didn't greatly matter whether she went or stayed. But to her the idea of going home and leaving—him—was almost agony.

She clutched spasmodically at the pine needles so that she winced at the sharpness of them, and he noticed the wince and took her hand and examined it carefully.

"Pine needles are sharp," he rebuked her, "and you should treat them with respect."

Then he patted her hand and placed it in her lap and smiled at her.

"I'm sure, being so very English, you are dying for your tea," he said. "Shall we sample the contents of that hamper?"

THE REST OF THAT AFTERNOON and early evening simply flew by. Virginia determined to enjoy every moment of it and to put all thoughts of the future right out of her mind, and together they drank tea out of a thermos, sampled all kinds of appetizing sandwiches and indigestible pastries and then packed up the hamper and went for a walk through the pine wood, ending on the little bridge which overhung the ravine so far below them.

Virginia looked into the ravine and shuddered a little as the realization hit her that but for the stout handrail they might easily become giddy and descend into the depths. Léon Hanson looked at her and noticed that she paled slightly as she looked downward over the rail. He put a comforting arm around her.

"There is no danger," he said, "but you obviously haven't a head for heights."

"Have you?" she asked, looking up at him.

"Oh, yes." He looked upwards at the majestic peaks soaring above and all around them. "One of these days I would like to take you mountain climbing with me, and then perhaps you will discover that after all you have a head for heights."

"I don't think so," she answered doubtfully.

But suddenly the thought struck her: with him no danger would actually be a danger—or it would cease to be a danger she could not face. She would cross Africa from north to south, enduring all the perils of the deserts and the privations and discomforts of fetid jungles if only it meant that he would be at her side. Anything—any price demanded of her would be better than that he should go away out of her life, or she out of his, as she obviously must in due course, and that she should hear within a short space of time that he had married Carla Spengler.

"What are you thinking of now?" he asked quite gently, staring down into her face.

Virginia knew she could not tell him what she was thinking, so she reminded him instead, "You said that before we left this pine wood you would ask a favor of me. What is it?"

"Did I put it as crudely as that?" he murmured and once again his eyes were drawn as by a magnet to the soft, tender line of her lips. "Something to remember this very pleasant day by would certainly sound much nicer!"

And before she fully realized what he intended to do he had bent and touched her lips firmly with his own.

Virginia did not draw back—and she certainly did not gasp, or utter any little sound of astonishment. She merely gazed at him with her wide gray eyes, and the expression in their depths was quite unreadable.

Dr. Hanson made a quick movement with his hand and lightly brushed a stray curl back from her forehead, tucking it beneath the yellow ribbon. And then he smiled at her very charmingly.

"Do you know," he said, "I've been wanting to do that for quite a while—certainly ever since we started off this morning!" Then he turned and let the way off the bridge. "I think we'd better be starting back now, especially as we've got to hand in that hamper at the hotel where we had lunch. We might if we're not too late, stay and have some dinner there, but, on the other hand, I've got a kind of feeling that I ought to get back—"

"Of course," Virginia said quickly. "You musn't let me take up too much of your time."

"Nonsense!" He was holding a straggling pine branch out of

her way and still smiling at her. "You've given up a whole day
to me and it's been wonderful."

It had been wonderful, but already they were on their way
back to reality and Virginia knew that she was keeping black
depression at bay by a tremendous effort. He slid into the seat
beside her and started up the car, and because she felt that he
must never guess how she was feeling—and he *had* given her
this one perfect day to remember—she began to chatter to him
brightly, almost too brightly, and he glanced at her a little
curiously before they started off on their homeward road.
And she kept up the chatter for quite a time, until they drew
near to the little mountain hotel where the fates who sit and
smile or frown at the daily doings of mortals decided that her
day was not to end just yet.

CHAPTER NINE

THE CAR HAD not been behaving in an altogether exemplary manner for the last mile or so and Dr. Hanson had begun to wear a faintly concerned expression. By the time they reached the hotel his black brows were frowning and the frown did not disappear when a garage mechanic at the hotel informed him that the fault could not be rectified in under half an hour at least. He decided that they would have to stay for dinner.

"It's not that I don't think dinner is a fitting way to round off this day," he told Virginia, "but I've remembered one or two things that I've deliberately forgotten all day and my conscience is not entirely at ease."

But nevertheless he tried to be a pleasant companion during the meal that was served to them on the same balcony where they had had lunch, and, sensing the effort he was making, Virginia played up and tried to be at her brightest, as well. But inwardly she felt a little sick because their spirits at lunchtime had been so naturally high, and now hers, at least, were at zero. It was no use pretending that they were having a good time because she could sense the impatience that was coursing through him—quite natural impatience, she realized, when one considered the preoccupations that were probably his—but a little damping to enthusiasms that were in danger of being completely extinguished from the moment they had left the bridge in the pine wood behind them.

Halfway through dinner he asked her to excuse him while he put through a telephone call to his house, and when he returned she could tell at once that the call had done nothing to dissipate his desire to be on his way. If anything, the impatient concentration of his brows was fiercer than ever and he answered abstractedly when the waiter inquired whether they wanted to take coffee on the balcony or inside the lounge of the hotel, as the shadows were deepening moment by moment and up here in the heart of the mountains there was a decided nip in the air now that the night was closing in around them.

"No, I don't think so," the doctor answered at last. "As a matter of fact, I don't think I'll take coffee at all." He looked across at Virginia. "It's going to be very awkward, I'm afraid, but the trouble with the car is much more serious than the preliminary inspection revealed, and it might be hours before it's ready for the road again. They've only got one car here that I can make use of, and it's so antiquated that I don't want to risk driving you back in it. If I break down, well and good, but if we were both stranded it would be much more serious for you."

"Then what—" Virginia looked up at him anxiously. It occurred to her that if they were both stranded on a mountain road she would be the last to offer up any complaints, but she hoped he could not read her thoughts.

"I suggest that you stay here for the night and when the car is ready tomorrow someone from the hotel can drive you back in it."

"I see," Virginia said, but she said it so flatly that he actually smiled a little.

"I'm sorry," he told her, and he leaned across the table and patted one of her hands as it lay beside the plate on which she had been crumbling a bread roll. The waiter, who was still awaiting orders about the coffee, discreetly averted his eyes, having already formed the opinion that since the celebrated Dr. Hanson brought this same young lady to the hotel twice on a single day he must be rather more than interested in her. "I'm really awfully sorry, but I'll have to drive fast and it would be most uncomfortable for you—"

"I wouldn't mind," Virginia answered, putting up a weak fight to be with him as long as possible.

"Wouldn't you?" he asked, lifting one of his dark eyebrows humorously. "Well, all the same, I don't think we should risk it, and they'll look after you well here. It's a very comfortable hotel from the visitor's point of view, and just now it isn't even half full, so you'll have a choice of rooms." He glanced down at his wristwatch. "As a matter of fact, I've had a visitor today who is still awaiting me at my consulting rooms, and I've simply got to dash away—"

"Oh, forgive me, of course I understand." And Virginia at once became cooperative, although the thought of being left alone at the hotel was a depressing one to her just then. "Please don't waste any more time. I'll be quite all right."

"You're sure?" He looked at her very earnestly.

"Quite sure!" She would have been glad to know that her smiling upward gaze at him gave away none of her true feelings.

A look that contained a certain amount of relief spread over his face.

"In that case I'd suggest that you have your coffee in the lounge and take your time over it. And don't hurry back tomorrow. Make the most of your brief stay in the mountains." He smiled at her encouragingly. "It will be quite all right if I have the car back by tomorrow night."

"I'll certainly see to it that you have it before then."

"Well, there's no hurry."

And then, with a casual wave of the hand he was gone, and she watched until his tall, slim figure in the dark blue blazer and pale gray flannels had disappeared through the doorway into the lounge.

The waiter bent a solicitous gaze upon her.

"*Mademoiselle* will take her coffee now? And she will, perhaps, take a liqueur, also?"

"No, no liqueur." Virginia fought hard to keep her tight little careless smile on her face. "Only coffee, please."

She spent the rest of the evening until bedtime sitting in the lounge and wading through piles of English, French and

Swiss magazines. And then, when the room seemed to begin to empty she decided to make acquaintance with her bedroom, and it was only when she had actually entered the elevator and was being borne upward that the realization that she had no sleeping things—not even a toothbrush—hit her. But a brief conversation with a highly intelligent chambermaid produced all that she needed, and Virginia sank her head onto her pillow at last with a strong sensation of anticlimax.

IN THE MORNING she wasted no time after breakfast before she ascertained that the car was ready for her, called for her bill and decided to return to Madame d'Auvergne without delay.

The bill, she discovered, was not her concern at all, for Dr. Hanson had left instructions that it was to be forwarded to him for settlement. The car was once more its smooth-running self, and she was driven by a member of the hotel staff who treated her with the utmost deference and deposited her at Aunt Héloise's villa in good time for lunch.

Aunt Héloise kissed her warmly and seemed concerned that she should have had to make the return journey alone. Perhaps an expression she recognized in Virginia's face disturbed her a little. It had something to do with hurt pride and was not the happy, anticipatory look she had seen in the girl's face before she had started off the previous morning.

"It was too bad of that naughty Carla to come back so unexpectedly and insist on seeing Léon last night," she said. "But for that Léon might have spent the night in the mountains too, although perhaps that might not have been altogether discreet. But it would have been better, I feel sure, if you had returned with him. I told him so, and I did not at all like the idea of your being alone in that hotel."

"Oh, I was perfectly all right," Virginia assured her, "and naturally Dr. Hanson was anxious to get back and see Miss Spengler."

Try as she would, however, she could not keep a faint trace of sarcastic bitterness out of the words. So it had been

Carla Spengler who refused to leave his consulting rooms and it was for Carla that he had dropped her, Virginia, rather like a hot brick!

Well, at least she knew now precisely where she stood with him! In future it would be easy—or, at least, easier—to decline any invitations he might feel tempted to hand out to her when he was feeling a little bored or Carla was not readily available.

On the pretext of washing her hands before lunch she went up to her room, and, almost weeping as a result of the excess of badly bruised pride she was suffering from—and something that was not as easily curable as hurt pride—she scrubbed at her lips with a face tissue in front of her mirror.

She hated, now, to remember that he had kissed her on the bridge in the dim green depths of the little pine wood, and that she had let him do so as if it was perfectly natural that he should exact a kind of toll for taking her out for the day.

Or had he perhaps regarded it more in the light of a reward for a good girl?

CHAPTER TEN

THAT NIGHT WHEN Dr. Hanson called his aunt and inquired whether Virginia had returned in safety from the mountains, although the evidence of his car having been restored to him much earlier in the day must have convinced him of that, Madame d'Auvergne did not let him know that Virginia was sitting near at hand in the mauve salon, although he asked to speak to her. A woman of high intelligence and tremendous understanding, she simply said that the girl was wandering somewhere in the garden and was probably difficult to find just then.

"I see," Léon said and seemed to ponder the matter. "But you'll let her know how very sorry I was that our extremely pleasant day should have been marred at the end of it like that, won't you?"

"Of course, Léon, *chéri*," Aunt Héloise murmured smoothly.

"And tell her also that the car I drove was a perfect brute and she would have detested it."

"Being a woman, she would probably have enjoyed the experience thoroughly," Aunt Héloise returned.

"Then women are beyond me!" he exclaimed, but he did not sound as if he was certain about that and there was a note of irritability in his voice.

"How is Carla?" Madame d'Auvergne inquired. "And when is she coming to see me?"

"Oh, she'll probably come and see you quite soon. Something went wrong with her engagements in America and she decided to cut them short and come home. She—" He broke off suddenly. "Are you quite sure Miss Holt is not anywhere about? I'd like to speak to her if you can discover where she is."

"My darling Léon," she reproved him, "This is Franzi's evening out and my rheumatic limbs will simply not allow me to go and search for her in the garden. I will give her your message."

"Very well." But he sounded a little short. "Tell her also that I saw her sister today and she is much improved."

"I will," Aunt Héloise murmured and replaced the receiver.

When she rejoined Virginia in the mauve salon she was smiling rather wickedly and she realized at once that Virginia had overheard every word of the conversation.

"I do not feel in the least guilty," the old lady confessed, "because for once in my life I told a deliberate untruth to my nephew. But somehow I did not feel that you would wish particularly to speak to him tonight—is that not it? she asked with a gentle note in her voice.

Virginia looked at her gratefully, wishing she didn't have to dig two teeth into her lower lip rather hard to stop it quivering. She nodded and then looked away quickly.

"It's silly, I know," she said, "but I really felt last night as if I was very, very badly in the way!"

Aunt Héloise leaned forward and patted her hand.

"A little matter of the pride?" she said understandingly. "But that feeling will pass, and—who knows—in the future we may arrange things more happily!"

Virginia could not quite follow what she meant, but if her hostess was suggesting that at some distant future date she and Léon Hanson might spend another day together somewhere then there was not the smallest hope of that. Once bitten twice shy was a commonplace saying, but in her case it was no more than the truth. In the future she would be more circumspect.

That night she more or less made up her mind to return to

England as soon as the travel arrangements could be completed. Lisa would be all right without her now, and in any case she had been away from home too long. It was time she came down to earth again and returned to the monotonous but undisturbed existence she had known before, and as she thought about it in the darkness and silence of her luxurious little bedroom at the villa, she suddenly felt wave after wave of genuine homesickness. Cromwell Road, her parents and her two brothers became, like the plum that is out of reach, the most desirable goal she could ever achieve, perhaps because she had not thought about them so much lately.

And as soon as her exercises were well started, and could be safely carried on by some experienced person in London, Lisa also would return home and then the family would be complete once more.

Virginia closed her eyes at last and thought how wonderful it would be when they were all together again.

In the morning she was so eager to explain to her hostess the necessity for her leaving without delay, especially in view of the fact that Lisa was to become her guest on the weekend, that she did not notice that a letter awaited her on the hall table until Franzi drew her attention to it.

Virginia regarded the envelope in some astonishment, for it was decidedly opulent and the handwriting was unfamiliar. Also, it bore a local postmark.

She opened it quickly and saw at once that it was from Mary Van Loon and had no connection whatever with Léon Hanson! She should have realized that the handwriting was strictly feminine and a very faint and pleasing perfume emanated from the envelope.

Mary Van Loon was apparently experiencing difficulties.

My small niece and nephew have arrived and I find it even harder to cope with them than I expected. They are a pair of pets, but—!!! Do you think you could come and have lunch with me today, if you have nothing more exciting on, and *advise me as to the best method of dealing with modern children*. You know you said it was very simple!

Do come if you can.

Mary Van Loon

Virginia had a curious feeling that she was being caught up in a web from which she might find it difficult to extricate herself later on, but Mary's letter was so warm and friendly, and despite its lightness, so appealing as well, that Virginia knew she would have to go to lunch with her at least. Perhaps the children would be so precocious that nothing would induce her to renounce her overnight plans and stay in Switzerland and look after them.

But something told her the children would not be precocious and that she might just as well have gone straight off to sleep last night instead of making up her mind, after writhing and tossing, to go home within a few days.

Lisa might go home within a week or so, but—

Well, the "but" could wait until she had seen Mary.

CHAPTER ELEVEN

AND MARY VAN LOON did little to persuade Virginia. It was the children who succeeded in doing that.

Precocious they certainly were, but they were also delightful. Paula wore a frilly frock that was not at all suitable for a child to play in, but with her golden curls and large blue eyes she looked both appealing and enchanting. Peter wore jeans and a checkered shirt, had a dagger in an ornamental sheath stuck through his belt, and regarded Virginia out of greenish hazel eyes that were much more unnaturally solemn than his sister's. He appeared to take a man's view of life.

"If you come here," he said, "I'll look after you, but you'll have to do a bit of looking after us as well. We've never had anyone to really *play* with us for long, you know," looking up at Virginia as if assessing her potentialities in that respect.

"What you want, young man," his aunt told him, ruffling his hair, "is someone to take you very strictly in hand and turn you into a respectable citizen."

Peter digested this for a moment and then slipped a hand into Virginia's.

"Will you come?" he asked earnestly.

Paula, who had been racing excitedly across the emerald expanse of lawn, came running back and slid both small, sturdy arms around Virginia's waist and hugged her.

"Yes, do come," she urged. "I like the look of you, and I'll be as good as I know how—sometimes—if you'll only come!"

"Well, there you are, you see!" Mary exclaimed, laughing. "Both the children *want* you to stay and look after them, I

don't know what I'm going to do if you *don't* stay, and
you're talking of going back meekly to England and taking
up a dull job for which I'm quite sure you're not in the very
least suited. Stay here and I can promise you it will never be
dull—not with these two around! You won't be treated like a
nanny—which always makes me think of a she-goat—and if
by any chance we go away from here you'll come with us.
And I'll pay you any salary you like to mention!"

"You're very kind," Virginia said and she sounded a little
wistful. It certainly was nice here on the Van Loon terrace,
which they had just reached after a tour of the beautifully
laid-out grounds. There were deep wicker lounging chairs
and little tables loaded with boxes of cigarettes and candies,
fruit and flowers. Everything and everyone was extremely
informal, including the servants, who had been brought
from America. She had been regaled with an almost perfect
lunch and now there was the magic shimmer of the lake
before her eyes, and all the splendor of the lakeshore. If she
went home to England she might never see such rare loveliness again. It was scarcely likely that she would meet with
such a charming friend and prospective employer as Mrs.
Van Loon, who had so far forgotten her dignity and almost
begged her to stay.

Then the salary, which she would insist should be no more
than the position warranted, would enable her to do things
for Lisa, who would be dependent on their father for a long
time yet, and altogether it looked as if she should accept.

"All right," she said suddenly, almost vehemently, "if you
really want me to do so I'll take on the job of looking after
these children."

Peter gave vent to a heartfelt "Yippee!" and Mary Van
Loon smiled.

"Lovely!" she said. "And how soon will you take it on?"

"How soon would you want me?"

"Immediately!"

Virginia was about to exclaim hurriedly that she would

have to tell her hostess all about it; that she could not run away and leave her at almost a moment's notice after all her extreme kindness to her, and that in any case she must have a few days to get together her things and prepare for this new venture.

And then she reflected that it would not be many days before Lisa would be leaving the clinic and arriving as a guest at Madame d'Auvergne's villa. That Carla Spengler was back and might be visiting Léon Hanson's aunt, and she had no wish at all to meet Carla while she was still accepting hospitality from Aunt Héloise. She could picture the raised, beautifully shaped eyebrows of the singer—the subtle inflection in her voice as she observed that Virginia had been a guest at the villa for quite a while!

There would be contempt in that voice, Virginia knew, and something very like open hostility, for from the first moment of their meeting Carla had shown no liking for Virginia. And Virginia would be made to feel that she had been taking advantage of her hostess's kindness and she would be rendered embarrassed and tongue-tied—especially if Léon Hanson was there, as well—and would want to creep away and leave the house....

She felt vastly inferior when Fräulein Spengler was around, and now, in addition, she felt bitterly envious of her....

But once safely entrenched behind the luxurious façade of the Van Loon villa she would find it a simple matter to avoid coming into contact with anyone she did not wish to come into contact with, such as Carla. For she would be tucked away in the nursery wing of the house and as an employee she would have a legitimate excuse for avoiding her employer's callers. Even Dr. Hanson, who was accustomed to walking into his aunt's house and finding her more or less waiting and ready to be noticed by him, could be avoided if she wished. Not that she would ever forget how much she owed to him, if the next few weeks proved that Lisa was going to

be the old Lisa again, but her gratitude need not take the
form of making herself into a kind of doormat for him to
walk upon.

He had been kind to notice her, to pay her the little
attentions he had paid to her. But in future she did not want
any more of those attentions. And now that Carla was back
his free time would be more strictly limited and the attentions would probably cease in any case.

Which, as she told herself, was exactly what she wanted.
In future her interests were going to lie with Mary Van
Loon's small niece and nephew and she would do her utmost
to reward Mary for the confidence she was displaying in
being willing to make this position available to her without
knowing anything at all about her capabilities.

SOMEWHAT TO MARY'S SURPRISE, therefore, she agreed to take
over the charge of the children just as soon as Mary would
like to have her, and they decided that the following day
would be ideal for them both if Madame d'Auvergne agreed.

Mary announced that she was going to drive Virginia
back to the d'Auvergne villa and she brought her smart little
cream-colored coupé around from the garage. The two
children insisted on clambering in, as well—they called cars
"autos"—and chattered like a couple of magpies while Mrs.
Van Loon was driving and made it difficult for her to
concentrate on the lakeshore traffic. Virginia in the end had
them both on her lap and realized it was no small handful
she had declared herself willing to be responsible for.

To Virginia's surprise Madame d'Auvergne did not seem
to think it at all strange that her young guest should wish to
leave her so abruptly, and instead she declared she was
delighted that Virginia was going to remain in Switzerland
and be near to her.

She insisted on Franzi's helping Virginia pack her things
and at dinner that night, which the two of them took in the
window of the mauve salon and without any visitors,

declared that she had formed the intention of giving a really large party to celebrate Lisa's recovery from her operation as soon as the young woman herself was in a fit condition to stand the excitement of it. They would have fairy lights in the garden, a quartet to play dance music, and if the night was fine perhaps even a cabaret out of doors. There would be quantities of champagne, a running buffet, culminating in a supper for which the Milano would make itself responsible, and altogether it would be a party to remember.

"And I shall *insist*," Madame d'Auvergne concluded, "that whatever the demands of this new employment of yours you will be one of my guests! I may even decide to give the party for both you and your sister, and on the whole I think that would be the better idea. For you have been such a nice guest that I hate to part with you," smiling almost tenderly at Virginia, "and I hope to see a great deal more of you in the future."

Her words made Virginia feel a little regretful—perhaps much more than regretful—that her stay in this restful villa had come to an end. And the thought that after tonight this quiet room, with its period furniture and elegance, would have given place to an up-to-date nursery, which a couple of lively charges would have the right to enter at any time, did for a few moments affect her like a depressing shadow.

In the future there would be no more relaxed evenings in a tapestry-covered chair while the radio played soft music and Madame d'Auvergne occupied herself with fine needlework or invited her guest to join her in a game of chess. No more listening almost subconsciously for the sound of the telephone in the hall preparing them for a brief visit from Dr. Hanson, or the brisk noise of his footsteps crossing the flagstone floor of the veranda. There would almost certainly be no more evenings on which she would stand side by side with Dr. Hanson down there in the moonlit garden, their elbows resting on the time-worn stonework of the balustrade that separated the terrace from the sparkling magic of the lake, while he gave her encouraging reports of Lisa. . . .

Virginia felt her breath catch for a moment at the thought that the last few weeks of her life had represented a distinct phase and tomorrow that phase would end. Whether the new one that was opening up before her would hold as much that she would be happy to keep hugging to herself for the rest of her days was impossible to tell yet.

Right up to the moment that she said her last good night to Aunt Héloise and went upstairs to bed, she knew that she was listening—and not subconsciously—for that soft ringing of the telephone in the hall that *could* have meant that Léon Hanson was coming out to visit them tonight. Or for the crisp, cool notes of his voice bidding them good-evening from the veranda door.

But he did not come and so far as she was aware he knew nothing of her plans. She had telephoned Lisa earlier in the evening to let her know what she was doing, and Lisa had sounded delighted.

"Oh, good!" she said. "Now you'll be staying in Switzerland more or less indefinitely? What does Dr. Hanson think?"

"I don't know," Virginia replied truthfully. "He doesn't know that I'm leaving tomorrow."

"Doesn't *know*?" Lisa sounded almost shocked. "But will he approve?"

"I can't see that it really matters whether he approves or not," Virginia replied quietly.

"But, Jinny, my sweet—"

Virginia interrupted hurriedly, "I'll get time off from looking after the Van Loon infants to come and take you away from the clinic on Saturday. Madame d'Auvergne is expecting you—"

"But Dr. Hanson has said that he will drive me to his aunt's house himself."

"Oh! Then I won't need to ask for time off. Well, take care of yourself, Liz."

"But Jinny—"

"Goodnight, Liz!"

"Goodnight, Jinny."

But Lisa went to sleep that night feeling faintly worried and uncertain in her mind about her sister. Virginia was usually such an uncomplicated person. But tonight she had sounded—how had she sounded—just a little bit distressed and—not particularly happy!

CHAPTER TWELVE

IT WAS SURPRISING how quickly Virginia, who had never before in her life coped with two such young children alone, settled down in the Van Loon household. The children were precocious, it was true, but in Virginia they recognized authority overlaid with a sweet reasonableness that appealed to them, and they never tried her too far.

They were also, she discovered, two rather lonely mites who lapped up affection like a pair of puppies, and Virginia was good at lavishing affection on children. She never tired of reading stories aloud or attending to small hurts or answering an endless stream of questions. Moreover she answered the questions to the best of her ability and this satisfied the children more than subtle evasions.

Peter was the more highly strung of the two, and of the two he made the most exacting demands on her. He was inclined to have nightmares and was also inclined to be fractious and irritable at times, and she exerted a lot of patience trying to sort out his problems for him. They were the problems of a naturally nervous child who had had very little settled home life, but he responded noticeably to Virginia's methods of dealing with him. He even began to copy her English accent, which amused Mary Van Loon very much indeed.

Mrs. Van Loon never interfered with Virginia's nursery arrangements. The children had lessons when Virginia decided they should and their daily outings and amusements were entirely her affair. It was something of a responsibility but it kept Virginia occupied, and that was what she preferred just then. She could also have as much time off as she wanted if she cared to take it, for she had been provided with an excellent nurserymaid who could take over when she went out, but her disinclination for going far from the villa somewhat surprised her employer, who had imagined that during the period of her sister's convalescence she would wish to spend as much of her free time with her as she could manage.

As for Lisa, her physical health had improved so markedly since her operation that she seemed to be romping back to a condition of complete bodily fitness. The exercises for her fingers had started and although it was early days yet there seemed little doubt that with perseverance, and if all went well with her otherwise, a bright and promising future would once more lie open before her.

She telephoned Virginia almost daily and Virginia gathered that in addition to the routine exercises to restore the suppleness to her fingers, the rest of her time was not allowed to hang heavily on her hands. Madame d'Auvergne was introducing her in all the circles where she had introduced Virginia, and everyone was being particularly kind to her. Clive Maddison was still exceedingly attentive, and she met him most mornings for coffee on the lakeshore. He had even succeeded in making such a favorable impression on Aunt Héloise that nowadays he had the right of entry to her villa at almost any time he wished.

Lisa's voice on the telephone sounded happy, confident and bubbling with enthusiasm about the future—although whether it was her future as a musician that meant more than anything else to her or a future that contained Clive Maddison, Virginia was unable to guess.

Lisa also was so full of gratitude to Léon Hanson that Virginia simply had to echo her enthusiasm—at any rate over the telephone. But alone in her sitting room-cum-nursery she tried not to dwell too much on him or recall how very nearly they had become really close friends.

Since leaving Aunt Héloise she had only seen him once and that was when she was taking the children for a walk. Peter and Paula were both happily eating ice cream after visiting a favorite café. They looked a quaint little pair, each clutching with a free hand a hand of Virginia's, and Virginia herself looked cool and a trifle remote in unadorned white linen with white sandals and slim bare legs that were rapidly acquiring a golden tan now that the weather was becoming increasingly warmer, and even verging on the unbearably hot at times.

But today there was a delicious breeze from off the lake and Virginia had the freshness of an English cottage garden rose. She looked particularly English, Léon thought as, driving his car along the lakeshore he suddenly caught sight of her and pulled in toward the curb.

"Well, well!" he exclaimed as their eyes met, and although Virginia's heart was hammering wildly she succeeded in preventing her expression from giving her away. In fact, the look in her gray eyes was so unrevealing that he stared at her rather hard for a moment, and if by any chance her color increased it could have easily been attributed to the warmth of the midday sun. "I must admit I was surprised when you ran away from Aunt Héloise without even letting me know about your plans, but I gathered it was to look after these children you left and not to shut yourself up in a convent! Does anyone have the pleasure of your society these days—apart, of course, from these precocious-looking infants."

But he smiled at the children in such an attractive way as he spoke that, after a moment of uncertainty, they each grinned back at him widely, their all-but-consumed ice cream suspended midway to their mouths.

"You appear to be enjoying yourselves," he observed. "Would you like another ice cream apiece? If so, hop into this car and I'll take you back to Franchini's, and perhaps Miss Holt will be good enough to drink a sedate cup of coffee with me?"

"Oh, no!" Virginia exclaimed quickly, preventing the children from grasping eagerly at the handle of the rear door. "They'll mess up your car with their sticky fingers, and anyway it's too near their lunchtime—"

"Nonsense!" he exclaimed, reaching behind him and opening the rear door himself. "In with you, you imps, and Miss Holt can come and sit beside me like a good girl!"

Virginia had no alternative but to do as he had more or less ordered her, and when he stared up the car she sat stiffly against the silver gray upholstery while Peter and Paula yielded themselves in a blissfully abandoned way to the thrill of being taken for a drive in this immensely superior big black "auto."

At Franchini's Virginia still could not prevent him from spoiling the children in a way that surprised her a great deal, for she had never thought of him like this before without any apparent care for his dignity or the dignity of his dark professional suit, and obviously enjoying himself in the company of the loquacious small American children. They chattered on so much and engaged his attention so completely that, to Virginia's relief, he had little opportunity to address any very pertinent remarks to her, until Peter and Paula became intrigued by a kite that someone had started to fly not very many feet away from them and almost in front of the open space where Franchini set out his gaily painted tables and chairs.

Dr. Hanson seized the moment to look directly across at Virginia and inquire, "Are you happy in this new job? You really like it?"

"I love it," Virginia answered, perhaps not altogether truthfully—but at least it was a very pleasant job.

He was silent for a moment, regarding her intently in that old, embarrassing way of his. And then, producing his cigarette case and offering it to her, he reminded her, "My aunt is giving a party for you and Lisa on the twenty-second. I hope you won't be too busy to attend?"

"Of course not," Virginia answered quickly. "Although I—" she paused and then hurried on. "Although I can't think why Madame d'Auvergne is putting herself to so much trouble on our account. It is more than kind of her, however, and I hope you will give her my—my love when you see her? Tell her that I miss our evenings very much!"

"I will," he promised in a detached, cool tone. "And I'm sure she'll be glad to know you enjoyed your stay with her."

"I did—oh, I did!"

And then, as it was almost one o'clock he offered to give them a lift home to the Van Loon villa.

He declined an invitation from Mary to remain for lunch, gave the children each a pat on the head and smiled coolly at Virginia. Without giving her another chance to say a word to him he was gone.

BUT VIRGINIA BEGAN to dwell upon the thought of the dance Madame d'Auvergne was enthusiastically planning to give. From Lisa, who continued to telephone her regularly, she learned that it was to be quite an impressive affair and that all sorts of preparations had already begun for it, although the night of the twenty-second was still two weeks away.

Madame d'Auvergne even talked about a firework display and the grounds were already being wired for the blaze of colored electric lights that were to dazzle everyone.

It was possible, too, that Carla Spengler would be persuaded to sing for them, and as, apparently, she had quite a remarkable voice, this was really something to look forward to.

Virginia secretly thought that she could endure it quite easily if the temperamental Carla decided, after all, against singing for the party. She knew that if Carla did sing it would probably be the bad moment of the evening for her, Virginia, for as Léon Hanson would almost certainly be among the guests she would have to witness the effect his all-but-fiancée's beautiful voice had upon him.

But the thing that concerned her the most was the dress she was going to wear when the big evening arrived. If the party was to be for her and Lisa then it was up to them both to look as good as possible, if only as a mark of their appreciation and their gratitude to their hostess. Lisa had already announced that she thought they would be justified in buying something new, particularly as their spending over the weeks they had been in Switzerland had been very considerably kept down because of the generosity of Madame d'Auvergne.

So, as Lisa had decided to have a new dress—and probably she had secret dreams of impressing Clive Maddison in it—Virginia also made up her mind that a new dress was important. The two girls met by arrangement at Franchini's café one afternoon, and after a cup of tea together— the first they had actually shared together in a restaurant since coming to Switzerland—they spent a delicious half hour examining the windows of the more exclusive little dress shops.

Lisa was so much like her old self and was so cheerful and carefree that Virginia found it difficult to keep her wondering eyes off her. But once inside one of the dress shops her whole attention became glued to the vital problem of what to choose, and like Lisa she began to wonder whether she would ever be able to make up her mind, because the selection was so tempting and bewildering.

At last, however, Lisa did make up her mind and Virginia heartily applauded her choice. Lisa in white could never be wrong—how often had Virginia seen her in the past, taking her seat before a piano in something that looked like the white wings of a moth—and white lace over a taffeta underskirt, with a drifting white lace stole to drape around her creamy shoulders when she wandered beneath the fairy lights in the garden on the night of the big event, was so perfect with her dark hair and eyes that it might have been created especially for her.

Virginia was torn between something that would make

her look slightly more sophisticated than she usually looked and something that she knew would really suit her. She had visions of Carla Spengler looking absolutely breathtaking in a confection that everyone would recognize as coming straight from Paris, and the thought of herself in the simple blue evening dress that she had worn so much lately made her shudder inwardly. No wonder a man like Dr. Hanson, who was accustomed to dealing with sophisticated women, and living in sophisticated surroundings, had treated her on the one occasion when he had taken her out for the day as if she were a youngster in her early teens who expected to be rewarded with some signs of affectionate appreciation.

Hence the kiss!

But she was trying hard to forget that kiss, and she concentrated ferociously on the dress the saleswoman was holding up in front of her. It was black net—almost as cloudy and attractive and distinctive as the one she had once seen Carla Spengler wearing. But of course she would not look like Carla Spengler if she wore it and Lisa was regarding it with a dubious expression on her face and seemed to consider that a pale pink—exactly the faint pink of a hedge rose—was more in her line.

"Not that I don't think you *could* wear black," Lisa admitted, studying her sister with her head on one side, "but you're not the sophisticated type, and black and sophistication do go together. However, if you're feeling very adult all at once and the pink does strike you as a wee bit little-girlish—"

"It does!" Virginia exclaimed almost fiercely. "It would make me look like a fairy on a Christmas tree."

"Mademoiselle would look quite delightful in the pink," the saleswoman murmured, visualizing those nut-brown curls, and those clear pink cheeks that were only a shade deeper than the pink of the dress itself above the wild-rose draperies. "Will she not try it on?"

But Virginia shook her head, suddenly determined.

"No, I've made up my mind to have the black!"

Not only did she buy the black dress but she bought herself dizzily high-heeled silver sandals to wear with it and some long, black net gloves that would come well above her white elbows. Lisa was regarding her with a faintly amused look on her face when at last they emerged from the shop.

"You are determined to cut a dash!" she exclaimed. "Is all this to impress Dr. Hanson?"

"Of course not!" Virginia exclaimed almost too hastily, and then was relieved to catch sight of a by now familiar figure on the sidewalk, who seemed to have chosen exactly the right moment to relieve them of the number of small parcels with which they were burdened. It was Clive Maddison. He was wearing white flannels and a blazer, which proclaimed that he had recently been playing tennis, and he had an unselfconscious grin on his face that Virginia liked the look of.

"But it does seem strange," she observed to him after he had announced that he was going to regale them both with the largest ice-cream sundae that they ever had in their lives, "that you always appear when you're most needed, as I'm quite sure Lisa has had opportunity to notice."

"Ah, but Lisa isn't the only one I make myself useful to," he defended himself, although his eyes were all for Lisa, looking rather like an ice-cream sundae herself in striped candy-pink linen with an enormous hat of white linen shading her piquant features. "I do occasionally make myself useful in other directions!"

This was so indisputably true that Virginia had to admit it at once, for of all the new friends she had made in that part of the world he was the only one who had endeavored to see to it that her decision to take up employment in their midst should not isolate her altogether from the life she had been leading. Mary Van Loon had a kind of genuine affection for him and whenever he appeared at her house he always sought out Virginia, and more than once he had come to her rescue when the children had been slightly above themselves while she had them out walking. He had even taken them off her hands while she kept an appointment at the hairdresser's.

He had an easy way with children; it was not quite the same thing as the way Dr. Hanson had with them, but at least he could make them obey him and he could keep them entertained, too.

So Virginia smiled at him in the friendly way she had when she liked anyone, and Lisa sat happily listening to him while he told them how full the hotel where he was now employed as an official tennis coach was becoming, and how little free time he expected to have to himself in the future—which was one reason why he was making so much of it now, looking meaningly at Lisa.

Lisa blushed and then didn't look quite so happy when the talk drifted to the forthcoming dance and her departure for home that was to follow it almost immediately. It had been arranged that, as her parents were anxious to have her at home again as soon as possible, her finger exercises should be continued in London under the supervision of an expert, and just as soon as permission was granted to her she would begin to test the results on her piano. Which did not mean as much to her as it would once have done; although for quite a different reason she was anxious to pick up the threads of her career where they had been forcibly dropped so many weary months ago now.

Virginia had a shrewd suspicion that her sudden desire to go ahead with her musical career was not unconnected with Clive Maddison and his own unsatisfactory attempts to carve out a career for himself. For if ever their friendship was to develop—as Lisa plainly wished it to develop, although what was in Clive's mind Virginia could only guess—then one of them must do something about making the future a little more secure. So Lisa was plainly fired with an enthusiasm that might otherwise never have taken possession of her again!

For all her liking for Clive, Virginia sometimes wished that he had not made his appearance on her sister's horizion at just this particular phase of her life.

He hired a taxi to drive them both back to their respective temporary homes, and having dropped Lisa at Madame d'Auvergne's villa—where both he and Virginia were persuaded to remain for a brief while and chat with Madame d'Auvergne—he went on to the Van Loon's with Virginia. At the foot of the terrace steps, with the children waving to them excitedly from the big glassed-in veranda, he said rather quickly, "One of these days I'm going to ask you to do something for me, if you will, Virginia."

"Why, of course," she answered, looking at him curiously. "But why me? Why not Lisa? Don't you think she'd prefer—"

"No." He shook his head quite decidedly. "I don't want it to be Lisa. You see, in a way it concerns Lisa."

"Mysteriouser and mysteriouser!" she murmured.

He smiled down at her engagingly.

"Then I can count on you?"

"Of course—if there's anything I can really do!"

"Good girl!" he exclaimed softly. "There is—I think!"

And then he ran back down the steps while the children continued to wave to him and Virginia wondered, with faint curiosity, what sort of service she was going to be called upon to perform for him when he decided that the moment was ripe.

CHAPTER THIRTEEN

BUT THE DAYS immediately preceding the dance were so fully occupied in her mind with thoughts of it that for once Lisa and her afairs slipped into the background and did not seem of quite such pressing importance.

One event that also sidetracked attention from Lisa during those days was the return of Edward Van Loon. He had been in so many European capitals in the past few months that he was a little weary, and he seemed delighted to find that his wife had found such a pleasing young companion as well as someone so eminently capable of looking after his small niece and nephew as Virginia Holt. And Virginia liked him on sight. She decided that anyone with those shrewd but kindly eyes was to be trusted absolutely and thought that although Mary had to pass so much of her time alone she was lucky to have acquired a husband who obviously adored her whenever he was near enough at hand.

The occasion of the master's return home was celebrated with one or two formal dinner parties, and one night Léon Hanson and Carla Spengler were among the guests. Virginia seized upon a quite legitimate excuse to absent herself. This excuse was provided by her small charge Peter, who had been restless and a little feverish all day and who declined even to think about settling down for the night unless she remained near him.

Mary, superbly dressed for the evening, looked around the night-nursery door and tried to persuade Virginia that it would be all right to leave him in charge of the girl whom Virginia herself had helped to train, but Virginia shook her head.

"I'd rather not," she said. "He's so highly strung and imaginative that he'll just work himself up if I leave him and in decidedly worse. When the family doctor arrived he diagnosed a severe chill but admitted that it might be the forerunner of something more serious, and they would have to wait to find that out.

Mary was quite horrified and began to take a firm stand. "Then it's no use your thinking you can nurse him," she said to Virginia. "We'll have to get a nurse in from outside and you must go and have a rest in preparation for his evening. Whatever you do you *musn't* disappoint Madame d'Auvergne and I don't want you to be disappointed, either. So go and put through those calls to the numbers Dr. Boulanger left with you and see if you can get a nurse to come out here straight away."

But although Virginia did her best she was very unwilling to yield her post to a stranger, particularly when Peter might not be so seriously ill after all. Children had a habit of running temperatures and then shaking them off just when you thought they had arrived at the crucial moment. And why should Mary Van Loon have to incur the expense of a nurse when it was Virginia's job to look after Peter?

But although she made genuine efforts to find a nurse who was free to attend without delay, they were efforts that were doomed to failure because no nurse was available until the following day. She reported to Mary, who had got on to the telephone on her own account, but without any better result. A nurse, efficient and highly trained, could arrive to take over the following morning but not a minute earlier. They would have to cope with Peter themselves in the meantime.

"Which means that I will stay and you will go to the dance," Mary said with great firmness.

Edward supported her. He had seen the dressmaker's box that had arrived for Virginia and the little rush of excited pink color to her cheeks when she took it from the maid Effie on the stairs, and he had pictured her trying the dress on in front of her mirror in her room afterwards. Virginia was the kind of woman who aroused the best in all really nice men and Edward Van Loon was really nice. He could quite happily forego the dance, and he and his wife would spend a any case I'm quite happy here. I've already ordered my dinner to be sent up on a tray and you don't have to give another thought to me."

"All the same, I shall," Mary hesitated, filling the nursery with the aroma of her Paris perfume. "Of course I could ask Léon to have a look at him, although he isn't our doctor, and he's such an important consultant that one doesn't like to do these things—"

"Of *course* not!" Virginia exclaimed quickly, horrified at the mere thought— she could imagine Carla Spengler's indignation if he were requested to ascend to the nurseries! "And as a matter of fact I don't think there's anything very seriously wrong with Peter. It's probably just a little cold and a slight rise of temperature, and once he drops off to sleep I'll slip in next door and make myself comfortable with a book."

"But won't you come down at all? Not for half an hour?"

"I'd rather not, if you don't mind."

Virginia smiled at her, thinking that her grooming was without fault.

"Well, if he isn't better tomorrow we'll have to get our own doctor. But I sincerely hope he is better because tomorrow night is the night of your dance and it would never do if you had to miss that!"

"No." Virginia could agree with her wholeheartedly about that because although she was almost grateful to Peter for his indisposition tonight, which had made it unnecessary for her to have to sit at a flower-loaded and intimate dinner-table with the glamorous and notable Carla and the man she was expected to marry and feel that she had no part or lot in the dinner-table conversation; tomorrow night was the night when she would wear her spectacular new evening dress, and in any case there would be lots of people and intimate conversation of any kind would be impossible. Besides, it would upset her very much if she had to disappoint Madame d'Auvergne after all the immense trouble she had taken and was probably taking at this very minute. "He'll be all right in the morning," she said optimistically. "I've given him half an aspirin and he's already much calmer," she said, laying her hand on the small, moist brow.

But in the morning Peter was not any better; in fact he was

Virginia sighed a little. Poor Lisa! How unfortunate that she had had to fall in love just at this time!

And then a thought even more incongruous lifted up its head. How unfortunate that she herself had had to fall in love at this time!

PETER, AS SHE HAD THOUGHT that he would do, sank after she had been sitting beside him for a while into an uneasy doze. His small hot fingers were tightly clasping the fingers of one of her own hands and whenever she made even the smallest movements he stirred and whimpered a little. But gradually his breathing became deeper and more even, the hot flush subsided in his cheeks and the clasp of that small hand grew less demanding.

In the next room Paula, whose bed had been removed in case there was a danger of infection, slept deeply and dreamlessly. Throughout the nursery wing there was utter silence, and the only illumination was the bedside lamp, which cast a pale golden light over the pastel blue bed in which the small boy lay and the still figure of the woman who watched him carefully.

Presently Virginia felt it was safe to remove her hand altogether and she stood up and wandered gratefully to the wide open window. How magical everything looked outside! The lake looked as if it were made of silver and the dark shapes of the trees that overhung it swaying a little in the night breeze. But it was such a gentle breeze that the night was almost oppressively warm and even the stars were not as bright as usual because of that atmosphere of soft and sensuous warmth.

But it was a night for dancing—a night for treading the scented paths of Aunt Héloise's garden and listening to the music of the orchestra playing behind banked-up masses of flowers. No doubt many couples would take advantage of the sheltered arbors and the quiet nooks where the sound of the music could still reach them, and they would be undisturbed by anthing else unless someone stumbled upon them by accident. Clive and Lisa would probably seek out one of those arbors. Or perhaps at this very moment they were standing side by side on the terrace, their elbows resting on the stone balustrade, just as Virginia had stood side by side with Léon Hanson when she was a guest of Madame d'Auvergne's....

Virginia had a sudden mental picture of Dr. Hanson and the golden-haired Carla stealing away from the crowd that thronged the d'Auvergne villa tonight and finding some little haven of peace where they could be sure of being alone....

Virginia moved restlessly. Peter now seemed to be sunk in almost healthful slumber and she went into her own bedroom, opened the doors of her wardrobe and took out the frock she was to have worn for the occasion. It hung suspended like a black cloud on her pink, satin-covered hanger and at the bottom of the wardrobe were the silver sandals she had purchased to wear with the dress.

It struck her all at once that she had been rather childish to wish to make an impression when she was not the type to do it. Not an unforgettable impression, anyway. Perhaps if she had listened to Lisa and chose the pink dress....

What other occasions would there be in her life for the wearing of this lovely, exciting black thing?

She carried the dress to her dressing table and held it up in front of her. A few moments later she was stripping off her utilitarian cotton and, with trembling fingers, drawing the black dress down over her shoulders. It settled with an altogether intriguing soft swish over her slender hips, and as she gazed at herself in the mirror of her dressing table her lips fell a little apart in pleased surprise.

It suited her! It did more than suit her; it transformed her! True, the pink-shaded light in her bedroom was highly flattering, but even allowing for the effect of the light she was something quite well worth gazing at. She even found it pleasant to gaze at herself.

Her skin looked so fair that it was almost startling, unless it was the sharp contrast afforded by the shadowy folds of material. And her lips seemed to be glowing and pulsating with life, and her hair, full of those dancing golden lights....

A sudden, slight noise in the adjoining room caused her to whirl around from the dressing table and move hastily in the direction of the door. Peter had been sleeping so peacefully but perhaps he was awake again....

And then she came to a sudden standstill in the middle of the night-nursery floor. Peter was still asleep and, so far as she could ascertain by a single glance, wearing almost a normal look, and he was still lying on his side with one hand tucked under his cheek. But the night-nursery door was open that is to say, the door that led to the corridor had recently been pushed open very quietly and carefully, thus accounting for the soft sound she had heard, and in the aperture the tall, slim figure of a man was standing, a man garbed in immaculate evening dress.

Virginia gazed at him and took in all the details of his appearance...white tie and tails...sleekly brushed hair as dark as the shadows into which it merged, an arresting, quietly arrogant face with a noticeable jaw and dark eyes that were politely questioning.

"What what are you doing here?" Virginia stammered.

"What are *you* doing here?" Dr. Hanson returned. "And why are you dressed like that? I thought you were behaving with extraordinary self-sacrifice, but you appear to be having a kind of dress parade!"

CHAPTER FOURTEEN

His tone was sufficient to prevent Virginia from being altogether overcome by her astonishment and a feeling of indignation took its place as she attempted to justify her somewhat odd attire.

"I— I was trying on the dress I would have worn tonight if I had gone to the party. There's nothing criminal in that, is there, as Peter already appears to be much better?"

He cast a barely perceptible glance at the bed, and then looked back at her.

"Why didn't you persuade Mrs. Van Loon to ask me to look at him last night?"

"Because I didn't think there was very much the matter with him last night. I still don't think there's very much the matter with him, but he's a highly strung and nervous child and already he depends on me a good deal. I wouldn't have been happy to leave him."

He nodded and walked to the bed and stood looking down at the sleeping child. Peter's attitude was completely natural now and he was breathing peacefully enough.

"I've come to relieve you, if you'd like to spend an hour or so at the dance?" Dr. Hanson astounded her considerably by telling her. "I don't propose to take over Dr. Boulanger's patient from him, but there are no rules relating to professional etiquette that can prevent me from acting as nurse for a short while. And if you can't put in an appearance at an evening's entertainment that is given expressly for you it will seem a little bit odd."

"Oh, but I do hope Mrs. Van Loon explained to Madame d'Auvergne—" Virginia began when he cut her short.

"Of course she did." He turned and looked her up and down quite coolly, noting all the things she had noted herself in connection with her appearance and perhaps a few other things that she had not been conceited enought to take note of, and that brought a sudden softened expression to the back of his keen dark eyes. "Your sister was concerned, naturally, because you had to absent yourself tonight and I've promised my aunt that you'll be with them in as short a space of time as possible. My chauffeur is outside and he'll drive you and as you seem to be all ready—"

"I'm not ready," she answered quickly. "I was merely trying on this dress, and in any case I couldn't possibly take advantage of your offer to stay here with Peter."

"Why not?" he demanded with one eyebrow raised.

She cast a look at Peter, who seemed to be stiring slightly, and he led the way out onto the balcony where they could talk without danger of disturbing the child. "Why not?" he repeated.

Virginia looked at him and all at once she knew why nothing would induce her to desert her post tonight and let Léon Hanson make it possible for her to enjoy the dance after all.

For one thing, there could be no enjoyment at the dance for her knowing that he was here—on that point there was no confusion in her mind! And another perhaps even more pertinent reason, had to do with the looks, indignant and supercilious, that she knew she would receive from Carla Spengler, who would consider her evening completely ruined for a very small cause. In addition to which she had no desire to ruin Dr. Hanson's evening—as quite obviously it would be ruined if he had to spend the best part of it separated from the woman he proposed one day to marry!

But she realized that she could not offer these excuses to Dr. Hanson, so she said, "Because I couldn't," and looked down at the skirt of the black dress and smoothed it mechanically.

Dr. Hanson frowned. "That is no reason," he told her almost impatiently.

Virginia lifted her eyes and met his boldly.

"Then perhaps you'll agree with me that it *is* my job to remain here and look after my charges when they happen to be ill? If one of your patients needed you you would scarcely consider a dance more important even if it was given by your aunt—or that's the opinion I've formed of you! And although I'm terribly sorry about Madame d'Auvergne and very much regret that I can't be there, there's nothing in particular I can do about it, is there?"

"Of course there is, you stupid child!" he retorted with a rough edge to his voice. "You can let me stay here while you enjoy yourself for a short time. I'm perfectly willing to stay so don't let's have any more argument about it."

"I'm not arguing," she returned with deceptive meekness, "but I couldn't allow you to stay here in my place."

"And if I insist on staying?"

"Then I shall stay as well!"

He took a turn up and down the balcony and then returned to her. "Go and put whatever final touches you want to put to your appearance, although you look all right to me as you are!"

"Thank you," she said to him demurely, "but if you don't mind staying with Peter for a few minutes while I get out of this dress and into something more suitable, I really will be grateful."

She turned toward the open glass doorway that led into the night nursery, but he got between her and the softly lit room behind him.

"Virginia!" He very rarely made use of her Christian name and there was something commanding about the way he did so now. "Virginia, you don't like me any longer, do you?"

For a moment Virginia was so surprised that she could say

nothing. Then, with her heart suddenly pounding, she stammered, "L-like you? Of course I like you! You've been very kind—done so much for Lisa—"

"Never mind Lisa just now," he interrupted, a hint of coldness in his voice. "But a few weeks ago you and I were rapidly becoming friends—real friends, I hoped! Until that unfortunate Sunday we spent together—"

"It was a very enjoyable day," she murmured mechanically.

"Was it?" He was staring hard at her with all the beauty of the night behind her and the moonlight making a silver web of her hair. "Was it so very enjoyable—for you?"

She answered with sudden honesty, "It was one of the nicest days I've ever spent in my life!"

"Oh, Virginia!" Instantly his voice and look softened softened almost miraculously. "And I've been wondering whether—whether perhaps it was because I kissed you? Whether you took great exception to that?"

Virginia put back her head and looked up at him.

"Why should I?" she inquired with a strange, cool note in her voice. "You were entitled to at least one kiss, weren't you, after such a very nice day? It was more or less your just reward. And it would have been most unreasonable of me to have objected!"

For an instant she almost recoiled before the further change in his face, the sudden, rather frightening whiteness that crept and played about his lips and the bleak hostility that banished the impetuous warmth from his eyes.

"So it was in that way you regarded it, was it?" he asked, and there was the chill of ice in his voice.

"And, naturally," she continued, "when you discovered that Miss Spengler was awaiting you at your consulting rooms you had to hurry back to her. Of course I understood that, too."

"Did you?" He seemed to be biting his lower lip hard. "And how did you know that Miss Spengler was awaiting me at my consulting rooms?"

For an instant Virginia hesitated.

"Your aunt told me when I got back the following day. But, of course," with a return of the sarcasm to her voice, "she understood, too, that it might have been a little awkward for you if I had insisted on being driven back in that car you borrowed and therefore you had no alternative but to leave me behind in the mountains. Miss Spengler might otherwise have thought it odd."

He gave her one long, curious, searching look and then turned away from her altogether. He walked rather stiffly to the balcony rail and stood looking out across all the unseen loveliness of the Van Loon garden and down to where the water rippled at the dock. His eyes became fixed upon the lake.

"I'm sorry I came here tonight," he observed in a voice that gave her no clue to what he was thinking. "Your friend, Clive Maddison, had already offered to take over your duties as nurse in order that you should not miss the party altogether when I decided that you might be more willing to yield your small invalid to me. But it would have been better if I had refrained from interfering and then Maddison might have been able to persuade you where I have failed."

Virginia was suddenly so shocked by all that she had said to him that she could not find her voice. It was just as if she were stricken dumb, and he gave her another quick look and then walked back into the night nursery. He went up to the bed where Peter was obviously sunk in healthful slumber and bent over him. Virginia saw him rest one hand lightly on the child's forehead and then he straightened.

"I don't think it's necessary for you to sit up with him any longer," he observed as she came up quietly behind him, just as if he were the local doctor who had merely looked in on his rounds and was giving instructions. "You're probably tired and you might as well go to bed. The child has no temperature any longer and in the morning I think you'll find him quite normal."

Virginia still said nothing and he grasped the handle of the white-painted door.

"Good night, Miss Holt. I wouldn't be too conscientious about your job in future if I were you, although it's an admirable thing to be conscientious. Don't bother to see me off the premises. I know this house well and I'll go out the way I came in!"

And before she realized it the door was closed quietly in her face and there was nothing but the subdued ticking of the nursery clock and a funny little sound between a half-snore and a sigh that escaped Peter as he made a convulsive move and turned right around on his pillows and then went promptly off to sleep again.

Virginia stood rigid for a moment and then quickly she reached out and grasped the handle of the door. The corridor was empty but she could hear footsteps running lightly down the stairs. She peered over the balustrade into the well of the hall below, but already the front door was closing with the same quiet precision with which the nursery door had closed.

A few moments later she caught the sound of a car starting up outside and she went back into the night nursery. She clasped her hands together in front of her, a gesture that was full of a kind of helplessness and was almost despairing, as well, and she said to herself hopelessly, *Oh, why, why did I have to say what I did to him? When he came here to do me a kindness! It was beastly, it was utterly horrible of me! And his affairs have nothing to do with me!*

She continued to clasp her hands together and she dug two white teeth into her lower lip so hard that a drop of blood spurted.

And after all that he's done for Lisa!

WHEN MARY AND EDWARD Van Loon returned in the small hours from a highly successful party on the lakeshore Virginia was still sitting huddled beside Peter's bed, only now

she was wearing her dressing gown. It was a dark red ripple
cloth, and it seemed to drain every drop of color out of her
face. There were mauve shadows under her eyes that made
Mary exclaim aloud in concern and there was something
more than tiredness in her eyes. She looked utterly dejected.

"My *dear*!" Mary exclaimed. "Why on earth didn't you go
to bed? And what happened to Dr. Hanson? He telephoned
to say that he was called to a patient and would rejoin us as
soon as he could manage it, but that might be any old time.
He also said he couldn't persuade you to leave Peter but that
Peter was much better."

"So he is," Virginia answered. A faint feeling of warmth
was stirring about her heart. "Do you mean that Dr. Hanson
didn't return to—to the party?" She nearly said "to Carla
Spengler."

"No, and his aunt was, for her, almost put out because
although she knows him so well she did think that on this
occasion, knowing the amount of trouble she had gone to to
make the evening a success, he might have dealt with his
patient more expeditiously."

Mary looked at her young governess somewhat curiously.

"Did he stay very long with you? And didn't you think it
was nice of him to offer to stay here with Peter?"

"Yes—it was very good of him!" But Virginia was experiencing a kind of wonderment, because instead of going
straight back to the party Léon must have returned to his
consulting rooms—and why did he waste so much time
when Carla was waiting for him? "But what about Miss
Spengler?" she asked. "Wasn't she disappointed as well as
Madame d'Auvergne?"

Mary permitted herself a kind of small, amused grim.

"She wasn't merely disappointed, she was positively livid!
From her point of view the evening was just so much waste
of time, and she even declined to sing because she said she
was suffering from a tired throat. Poor Madame d'Auvergne. And she was *so* sorry about you!"

"I was sorry, too," Virginia assured her. But she was so tremendously relieved that she wasn't the only one who had suffered private agonies during the course of that evening that she couldn't keep some of it out of her voice. "But I'm sure Lisa enjoyed herself thoroughly."

"Oh, she did. In fact, it was quite a wonderful evening." Mary yawned uncontrollably.

"But you, you poor sweet, you must have been extremely bored!"

"I wasn't exactly bored," Virginia told her truthfully.

"No?" Mary cast her another of her rather searching looks and then moved in the direction of the door. "Well, Edward is sending you up a glass of sherry that he absolutely insists that you drink before you go to bed, and I recommend that you go without delay." By the door she paused. "But I *would* like to know why Léon chose to absent himself altogether from this evening's party. It's true that he arrived for it, and he seemed in good spirits when he arrived, but a patient who could make him stay away for so many hours...."

"Perhaps it was an important patient," Virginia suggested, tucking in an end of Peter's sheet.

Mary thought that her face was a little too inscrutable.

"Perhaps it was," she agreed. And then she rather cast Virginia back into the depths where she had been before as she remarked, "Of course, there's no doubt about it, Carla means to have him if she can get him! She mightn't always have shown so much determination, but she does now. I wonder why?"

"Perhaps it has occurred to her that she could lose him," Virginia replied, thinking with a sick feeling at the base of her stomach that any woman would be a fool to risk losing a man like Léon Hanson when by fighting for him she could **gain possession** of him for the rest of her life. It was only when there was no chance at all of sharing even a small part of his life that it was useless to fight.

CHAPTER FIFTEEN

DURING THE next few weeks it became increasingly clear to Virginia that if ever she had stood the chance of gaining the friendship of Dr. Hanson—and even friendship was worth having when the thought of living without it was like being forced to exist in a waterless desert—that chance was gone forever.

With the return of Lisa to England, and as the result of a decision taken suddenly by Madame d'Auvergne to spend a few weeks with an old friend in Paris, the only two links she still had with the doctor were swept away and she saw little or nothing of him. Even Mary Van Loon, who visited at most of the houses where he visited, reported that he was rarely come upon nowadays. He seemed to be increasingly busy at the clinic and what little spare time he had was devoted to Carla Spengler. And Carla was contemplating a second trip to America and was trying to persuade him to accompany her!

Was it a honeymoon trip that she was doing her best to persuade him to take with her. Virginia wondered.

But before Lisa left and Madame d'Auvergne flew off to the Paris she loved, Virginia did see him for a brief while at a very informal little tea party that Aunt Héloise gave for Lisa.

He walked in when they were midway through sampling the host of dainty sandwiches and little cakes that Aunt Héloise had provided for the occasion and accepted a cup of tea that he did not, however, drink. He was particularly nice to Lisa and sat beside her on one of Madame d'Auvergne's striped Empire couches, and gave her a lot of helpful advice about the various things she should and should not do in the immediate future. He urged her to persevere with her exercises and advised her to be patient and wait a little while before attempting seriously to play her piano again, warning her with a smile in his eyes that he would expect to be notified of her first big recital and adding that if it was humanly possible he would be amongst her audience.

Lisa was plainly almost overcome by her gratitude, but she was happy and bright and confident about her future. Only Clive Maddison, standing beside the window and gazing out rather glumly across the garden, did not appear to share her confidence.

Virginia, to whom Dr. Hanson barely addressed a word, gravitated after a while over to the window also, and Clive pushed the glass doors open and invited her to accompany him outside. Together they descended the steps to the lawn.

Clive was drawing furiously at the end of a half-smoked cigarette and he suddenly flung it away into a flower bed and scowled as he produced his case from his pocket. He passed it to Virginia but she shook her head.

"No, thanks," she said. Then she told him reprovingly, "You're smoking too much, Clive! I've noticed it particularly lately and the tips of your fingers are becoming quite noticeably stained. And, anyway, it's expensive."

"It is," he agreed, "it's confoundedly expensive— everything's expensive when you don't really earn enough to keep yourself in socks, let alone support a—wife!" His brows were meeting above his brilliant blue eyes and they were staring harshly at the lake.

"I'm sorry," Virginia murmured, touched by something hopeless in his voice which had never been there before. "Are you and Lisa parting merely good friends or are you hoping to see one another in the future?"

"We're certainly not parting *friends*," he bit out, "and we're hoping to meet again just as soon as it can possibly be arranged!" He stood still suddenly and looked down at her, his hands thrust deep into his pockets. "Virginia, you're the only person who can help us and I had your half promise several weeks ago that you would if you could!"

"Well?" She looked up at him. "In what way can I help you?"

He took her by the arm, after glancing back quickly over his shoulder to make sure that they were not being followed, and maneuvered her into a cool green arbor overlooking the lake, where they were scarcely likely to be disturbed.

"I'll tell you," he said, providing her with a chair and taking another beside her. "I want you to have dinner with me at the Milano tomorrow night. Lisa leaves in the morning, and I shall be glad when she's gone, because at this stage she's not really fit enough to be brought face to face with anything in the least likely to prove unpleasant."

"I quite agree," Virginia said. "But is there any unpleasantness that she's likely to be brought face to face with?"

"Well, it's not really likely but—" He smiled rather ruefully at Virginia. "I don't want to tell you everything just now," he admitted, "but I'm expecting a visitor tomorrow who will be staying at the Milano—a visitor from England. If Lisa had been one hundred per cent fit I'd have been delighted for her to meet him, and I can't imagine any man—least of all one who was once very impressionable, to say the least, if all that I've heard about him is correct—not being knocked completely sideways by Lisa and her big dark eyes. They reminded me of the eyes of a startled fawn when I first met her. She's so full of strange, unworldly charm and sweetness—"

"Yes, yes," Virginia said, interrupting him not because she was in any way averse to listening to this catalog of her sister's various attributes, but because she had a feeling that their absence would be noted and if not commented upon, almost certainly misconstrued in one quarter at least. "But where is all this leading us? Don't tell me you want me to impersonate Lisa?"

"Of course not," Clive reassured her at once. "But as Lisa's sister—a genuine representative of her family ...." And then he broke off and shook his head. "I want you to trust me, if you will, and I promise you my scheme is perfectly simple and is not in the least likely to recoil upon you. And you *may* be doing an immeasurable service to me, and what must be more important to you, to Lisa—"

"And all that it involves is that I dine with you tomorrow night at the Milano?"

"That you dine with me *and* my—my friend!"

Virginia thought quickly. She could quite easily get the evening off she knew, for a free evening was certainly due to her and she was faintly intrigued by this extraordinary invitation, and anything that she could do for Lisa she would do. But the Milano! The Milano was smart and it was now the height of the season and what would she wear?...

She thought of her black dress, but that might be a little oversmart for a simple dinner party.

"Would you wish me to look my best for this occasion?" she inquired. "Because my wardrobe is strictly limited and I've only one good dress, which might or might not be suitable—"

"If it's the one you were to have worn on the night of Madame d'Auvergne's dance and that I've heard about from Lisa, then wear it," he answered her, smiling. "I understand you really launched out for that occasion and it was a thousand pities you weren't able to be there. But I was fully prepared to take over your job as night nurse, only that fellow Hanson never allowed me the opportunity."

"Yes, it was kind of you," Virginia said quickly, gratefully. "Dr. Hanson did tell me."

"Oh, he did, did he?" He gave her a rather curious look. "He's an odd fellow at times, Hanson. Quite unshakable when he makes up his mind, and he made up his mind on the night of the party that he was the one who was going to relieve you, although I don't think his lady friend, Miss

Spengler, was entirely appreciative of the consideration he showed for you. She was a little bit peevish afterward, anyway."

Virginia said nothing, although any mention of Léon Hanson made her heart quicken its beat uncomfortably these days, and then she thought she heard footsteps coming along the path toward them and she looked up quickly. Clive said persuasively, "Then you *will* dine with me tomorrow?"

"I will if you really want me to."

"Good! Then I'll pick you up about a quarter to eight—"

"Oh, so there you are!" Lisa's voice exclaimed lightheartedly as she made her appearance around a bank of shrubbery. She smiled at Clive. It would never have occurred to her to feel in the least suspicious because he and her sister were apparently enjoying a quiet tête-à-tête together, but her companion, Dr. Hanson, who walked just behind her had a look on his face that caused Virginia's heart to sink like a plummet. Was there, she wondered, a faint hint of contempt in his eyes as he glanced at her or was it purely her imagination?

"Your sister is making an early start tomorrow morning, so I advised her to spend a quiet evening and go to bed early," the doctor observed in his incisive tones to Virginia. "You'll probably want to spend a little while alone together, so if I can give you a lift back to your hotel, Maddison...?" he asked with a bleak, unfriendly look at the tall Englishman.

"Thanks very much," Clive replied quite imperturbably, "but I shall walk back later on. I'm not in any hurry."

Léon Hanson's chiseled lips seemed to tighten a little and the expression in his dark eyes was suddenly inscrutable as they rested upon Virginia.

"Then I'll say goodbye to you, Miss Holt." But he did not attempt to touch her hand, although there was something like an ache in her cold fingers as they waited for even that fleeting contact. "And a happy return to your family circle to you, Lisa!" he said, quietly gripping her hand.

Lisa's lower lip quivered noticeably and a sudden tear spilled over and ran down her cheek, which was still a trifle wan.

"Thanks to you, it *will* be a happy return!" she whispered.

"I'm sure it will," he replied, and his warm and comforting smile was for her alone.

When he had left them, walking briskly away to his car, all three stood silent for perhaps half a minute listening to the subdued noise of his engine starting up and then Lisa turned impulsively to her sister.

"I wish I knew why he isn't *quite* the same," she said. She stared hard into Virginia's face. "He isn't the same to you, Jinny!"

"Isn't he?" Virginia appeared astonished. "Don't you think you're inclined to let your imagination run away with you, Liz, my dear? Dr. Hanson is an extremely busy man and I just happen to be *your* sister! He's made a most satisfactory job of you and there's no reason at all why he should waste any more time on me."

"But at one time I thought—" Lisa bit her lip, and then she gave vent to a little sigh. She was obviously perplexed by Virginia's apparently quite natural smile and by her air of being a little amused. "Oh, well, so long as you don't mind— and I must admit that glamorous creature Carla Spengler is quite something! If he marries her they'll be a very attractive pair, for he *is* attractive, and perhaps she'll make him happy. But he doesn't look terribly happy at the moment."

And then she looked at Clive and Virginia realized what she was thinking. Their last night! And they must have so much to say to one another!

"I'll go and have a chat with Madame d'Auvergne," she said hastily. "I haven't had much opportunity to do so lately and she's going away soon. But you must remember what Dr. Hanson said to you, Liz—you must go to bed early."

"I'll see that she goes to bed early," Clive answered for her very quickly. And then he took her almost roughly by the hand. "But first she's coming with me to have a look at the lake!"

THE NEXT NIGHT, when Clive called for her at the appointed time, Virginia could see that her appearance took him by surprise, despite the fact that he was looking and obviously feeling downcast because Lisa was no longer in Switzerland.

"My word!" He put his hands on her shoulders, turned her around and she saw the honest admiration in his eyes. "No wonder women spend such a lot of time worrying their heads about clothes! Before you were a very attractive young Englishwoman—exceedingly English! Now you're almost too exciting to be English!"

Mary Van Loon, who had also spent some time admiring Virginia, came forward to greet him in the hall before they left for the Milano and there was a teasing look in her eyes as she lifted a warning finger.

"I hope you won't forget that Lisa has scarcely touched down at Heathrow Airport! And please don't let this be a flagrant case of off with the old and on with the new!"

Clive grinned at her.

"Nothing of the sort," he assured her. "Virginia and I have business to discuss, that's all!"

Mary elevated an amused eyebrow.

"Well, it's a very good dress to discuss business in, anyway," giving a little pat to the cloudy dark stole that was all that protected the girl's slim white shoulders from the caress of the warm night air. "It should give you confidence if nothing else."

And Virginia felt that she needed confidence when once more she found herself ascending the steps of the Milano and entering the brilliantly lighted vestibule. The last time she had descended those steps Léon Hanson had been at her side, his arrogant head in the air while he led the way out to his car, and she had been new to Switzerland and everything had been touched with a hint of magic.

But now the magic was no longer there, somehow, although the hotel was as luxurious as she remembered it and obviously crowded to capacity. In the great glassed-in veranda, which overlooked a kind of central courtyard where a fountain played, sending diamond spray high into the rose-flushed air—for the sun was just about to disappear into the lake, crimson as blood—and masses of exotic plants bloomed in ornamental tubs and stone vases, people were drinking cocktails and laughing and displaying the tans they had acquired during the golden hours of daylight. And the women without exception were tremendously smart and the men were beautifully groomed and attractive in black and white.

Clive, as faultless in his appearance as any man among them and better-looking than most, with that indefinable air which never deserted him and set him apart as unmistakably English, led her to a table where there were two other chairs and where a waiter hastened to take their order for drinks.

"You'd better have a sherry while we're waiting," Clive said. When it arrived he put it into her hand and lifted his own glass. "Let's drink to the success of this evening!"

Virginia obediently lifted her glass.

A twinkle came into Clive's eyes.

"I think we should drink to you, too, in that dress—and the exciting future that must one day await you!"

"Hear, hear!" said a somewhat gruff voice behind them, and Virginia very nearly dropped her sherry as she looked up into the intensely shrewd eyes—very blue eyes they were, like Clive's—of an unusually tall elderly gentleman with white hair and a fierce white mustache, who was gazing down at her through a monocle, which sat securely in front of his right eye. "Hear, hear!" he repeated. Then he said briskly, "Present me to this young lady, Clive!"

Clive obeyed with alacrity.

"Miss Virginia Holt, sir!" He looked with apology across at Virginia. "Miss Holt—Virginia—let me introduce my father, General Maddison."

CHAPTER SIXTEEN

"WELL, WELL, WELL!" boomed the general when at last he had installed himself in the spare chair at the table, stretching his long legs out in front of him as if in disdain of the cramped accommodation the chair afforded him. His monocle was still in place and he made no attempt at disguising his study of Virginia; indeed, he carried it out with a good deal of zest and obvious approval. "You certainly know how to pick 'em, my boy! And if this one's anything like the other one, the one you want to marry—"

Virginia felt herself blushing almost to the tips of her small, shell-like ears where a pair of dainty pearl studs— presented to her while she was dressing that evening by Mrs. Van Loon as a mark of appreciation she said, and on condition that she wore them and didn't hide them away in a trinket box—gleamed against her pink skin. But Clive did his best to come to her rescue.

"You musn't embarrass Miss Holt, sir—she isn't accustomed to these open tactics, and in any case Lisa isn't a bit like her. Lisa's dark, while Virginia's fair—"

"Always did prefer a blonde myself!" the general exclaimed with a wicked little wink at Virginia, and then he examined the contents of their glasses and uttered a snort of disgust. "Sherry! I hope you don't expect me to follow your example and drink that! There's nothing like a whiskey and soda at this hour of the day. Hey, waiter!"

While he was issuing his instructions to the waiter Clive leaned forward and attempted to mitigate any sore feelings Virginia might be nursing because he had allowed her to be so ill-prepared for this meeting, and for a certain amount of ordeal that lay ahead of her.

"I didn't want to let you know in advance that it was my father you were going to meet because I wanted you to be entirely yourself and not prepared to meet someone who might alarm you a little. And although I'll admit the Old Man is a bit alarming at times, he's not really the least bit tough at heart. The only one he ever decided to get tough with was me and I expect I richly earned it. However—" he said with a wry twist to his lips "—the important thing is that I felt from the beginning that he'd fall for Lisa, as it's quite obvious he's already fallen for you. And although it's five years since we met—"

"Five years is a long time," the older man observed, catching the tail end of the conversation after sampling his whiskey appreciatively. "A very long time when you've only got one son, and he persists in roaming like a gypsy about the globe without a thought for those he's left behind!" He glared at Clive, an angry flash in his blue eyes under the bushy white eyebrows. "You've got a lot of talking to do, my boy, before you're going to convince me that you've had a change of heart and want to come home and try an honest job of farming for a change. At one time you despised farming—"

"I don't think I despised farming, but I didn't think I'd make a good farmer," his son corrected him, a whimsical gleam in his eyes. "There's a subtle difference, you know."

"Well, there may be a subtle difference, but if there is it's too subtle for me to follow. All I know is that you cleared out—you didn't want anything as dull as farming, although apparently your wanderings about the world have not resulted in your making your fortune."

This was so undeniably true that Clive could do nothing but admit it, and Virginia flashed him a sympathetic glance as she detected the wry note in his voice. The general uttered a few hoarse noises and then glared at him afresh.

"And now you want to come back to High End and I'm not at all sure that I want you back at High End!" However, he produced his pocket handkerchief and blew his nose violently for several seconds, after which he admitted, "But your Aunt Hetty's more sentimental than I am and she's already preparing to kill the fatted calf to welcome back the prodigal! Making all sorts of plans, too, which I think she's a fool to make—but women are fools!"

He grinned at Virginia, not so much apologetically as in almost a puckish, schoolboy fashion, and she smiled back at him with a sudden feeling of relief for Clive—and, of course, Lisa as well—because she was suddenly certain that this seemingly fierce old man was not really at all fierce at heart. Not nowadays, anyway. He might have been at one time, when he and his son first began their differences, but possibly being without his son—and feeling intensely lonely at times—had brought about a change of feelings.

Clive seemed much touched by the mention of his aunt.

"Good old Aunt Hetty!" he observed. "I could always depend on her, and even during these years when I've been roaming, as you put it, sir, about the globe, she's never omitted to write to me at least once a month."

"That's why I say the woman's a fool," the general told him.

But Virginia leaned forward quickly.

"Oh, no," she said softly, "oh, no, she isn't, General Maddison! And women are not really fools, you know! They're only more intuitive than men and much more prepared to forgive and forget."

"Is that so?" the general inquired with a twinkle in his eyes and then he pushed back his chair. "Well, you can let me have your views on this subject while we have dinner, but I object to taking my meals in an overcrowded dining room and that's what it's going to be like if we delay much longer."

With old-fashioned courtesy he offered her his arm until they reached their table, and when they did so Virginia saw

that it was in quite a prominent position near the center of
the huge room, and that it was decorated with some exceptionally choice dark red roses. Had they, she wondered, been
ordered specially by Clive? And if so what a pity it was that
Lisa was not here in her stead to appreciate them.

Champagne was already cooling in an ice bucket beside
the general's chair and he directed his attention to it from the
moment that he handed over his strong, gold-banded
cane—without which he was seldom seen, being, he
declared, a martyr to gout—to the care of the waiter and had
Virginia installed in the chair on his right hand.

He toasted her with extreme dignity as soon as the champagne had been poured into the three glasses, and then
settled himself to enjoy what was plainly going to be an
excellent dinner.

Whether it was the effect of the champagne or whether
there really was an almost complete lessening of tension as
the meal progressed Virginia could not be sure, but by the
time the dessert course was reached she actually began to
feel that she was glad she had accepted Clive's invitation.
Her own concerns had for the time being ceased to be of any
major importance, and the general, she had made up her
mind by that time, was really charming. He might have an
embarrassing twinkle in his eyes and his manner was decidedly martial and his voice was so loud and penetrating that
she felt sure that at moments it was heard in every corner of
the room, but he had a lively sense of humor and under-
neath his occasional brusqueness she sensed a genuine kindness. And he certainly paid her a good deal of attention. He
told her more than once that if her sister was anything like
her he would look forward to meeting her, which certainly
pleased Clive, who also began to look somewhat more at his
ease as they waded through course after course.

And after that one little outburst while they were having
drinks on the veranda the general made no further reference
of any kind to his son's defections. Instead it looked very

much as if, having established contact with him again, he was not even dwelling on any past lack of consideration and was prepared thoroughly to enjoy his own evening and his visit to Switzerland.

This made Virginia happier than she had been for a long time, if only because it looked as if things might work out well for Lisa.

An orchestra played soft music in the enclosed courtyard adjoining the dining room and couples were dancing when they left their table and had their coffee on the fringe of the open space beneath the starry night sky. The lighting effects were highly flattering to feminine frocks and complexions and Virginia, in her black dress with her eager eyes and vivid mouth and pretty, soft hair, was as appealing as any woman who danced or looked on at the dancing.

Not that Virginia looked on for very long, for the general, despite his gout—which was perhaps not quite so troublesome for the moment—insisted on being the first to escort her out on to the dance floor and she found that he was a very adequate performer. Then Clive asked her to dance, too, and as it was a waltz and a favorite and popular tune, Virginia thoroughly enjoyed it. When she returned to her seat on the edge of the floor her eyes had a happy sparkle in them and there was a most attractive soft color in her cheeks.

The lights went down for a floor show and she leaned forward to watch it with the enthusiasm of one who was not often allowed the chance to witness this kind of spectacle. The dancers wore Swiss national costume and the yodelers' voices thrilled her. With that width of night sky like purple velvet sewn with stars above her head, and the glimpses of snow-capped peaks on all sides of her, this was something she knew she would always remember! She looked a little bemused when the lights went up again and the pair of eyes watching her from a neighboring table did not immediately affect her with the awareness that she was being watched.

But when, inevitably, they did draw her gaze like a
magnet, her heart gave one of its tremendous bounds and
then she went quite alarmingly pale. The general was
clapping the floor show heartily and at the same time he
commenced a dissertation on a subject that was very dear to
him, namely Simla in the days when he had been a subaltern,
and the displays of native dancing that had intrigued him at
that time, but Clive noticed the sudden alteration in
Virginia's looks and the direction in which her gaze had been
drawn. And he looked, too, and saw—not altogether to his
amazement—that it was Dr. Hanson who was sitting back in
one of the gilt-legged, rather spindly chairs, and proclaiming
all the advantages of a first-class tailor who had fitted him
out with his evening things, and staring at the same time very
hard and rather bleakly at Virginia.

Beside him at the little table on which were liqueur glasses
and coffee cups was Carla Spengler, wearing something that
was spectacular and infinitely suited to her golden glamour.
The effect was heightened by brilliant emerald earrings, an
emerald bracelet and a pendant that blazed like green fire on
her faultless neck. She looked a little bored—even a little
peevish—and Dr. Hanson wore an expression that recalled
to Virginia's mind those sculptured marbles she had seen in
museums, which always suggested a remoteness and lack of
kinship with ordinary commonplace human beings.

It was not so much a detached expression as one that was
deliberately withdrawn. It provided no clue whatsoever to
the thoughts that lay behind it or the sensations that must
exist somewhere beneath that elegant black and white exteri-
or. He was not even smoking a cigarette as he sat very still
and studied, with those strange, inscrutable eyes, the
reactions of the woman in the black dress, who had been so
obviously and genuinely enjoying herself up till now.

Clive exclaimed, "Hello, it's Hanson!"

"And Fräulein Spengler," Virginia murmured mechanically.

"Who? Where? What?" The general was gazing about him, full of the Englishman's desire to do the correct thing and be hospitable if necessary. "Friends of yours, Clive? Then introduce them!"

Clive cast a quick glance at Virginia's face as if silently asking whether she would approve of this or not, but Virginia was in no condition to respond to a tacit appeal of this sort even if she understood it, which was doubtful. The sight of Léon Hanson and the woman everyone expected him to marry had had the effect of dissipating all her calm enjoyment of the evening, and it was as much as she could do to appear natural as Clive walked over to the other table and invited the two who sat rather stonily there to join them and meet his father.

But Dr. Hanson rose immediately to the situation and with Clive's rather awkward explanation that his father would be delighted to make the acquaintance of the surgeon who had worked with such skill upon his own battered person after his skiing accident, the doctor stood up easily and went quickly across to meet the general, giving him one of his pleasantest smiles as they shook hands.

Carla, no doubt because Clive was so very personable— and perhaps also because her evening had been falling a little flat for some reason or other—smiled at him graciously and was unusually affable to General Maddison after she had been introduced to him. She was sufficiently a snob to recognize that although the son might have become somewhat impoverished of recent years and found it necessary to earn his living in a way that most of her friends considered a little below the dignity of one they received into their intimate circles, the father had obviously a good deal of substance behind him and had something besides that was even more important than substance and could never fail to command respect.

Virginia received a cool little nod from Carla and was thereafter ignored by her almost completely, but Dr. Hanson crossed over to her side and sat in a chair and talked to her. His talk was along the most conventional and somewhat frigidly polite lines, but whenever she lifted her eyes she saw that he was looking at her and there was something in his look that set her mentally groping for an explanation of whatever it was.

He seemed almost to be trying to probe her mind and read her thoughts, and yet he sounded detached and even uninterested as he persisted with his flow of unimportant small talk. He did not so much as mention Lisa.

At last he asked her whether she would like to dance. Carla had made it plain to Clive that she would like nothing better at that moment than to dance a tango with him that the orchestra had just struck up, and they were out on the floor with the singer moving superbly in the sensuous motions of the dance and Clive guiding her movements with just as much skill. But Virginia knew that she had none of that skill when it came to dancing the tango and she more than suspected that Léon Hanson was as accomplished as Clive. Moreover, she had an extraordinary sensation amounting almost to panic at the very thought of dancing with him and although he could not know it her fingers were cold with dread and something inside her was trembling uncontrollably in case he should insist. And then what? How would she feel and behave if he did insist?

But he did nothing of the kind. If he disbelieved her excuse that she had acquired a blister on her heel and had made up her mind to dance no more that night, he did not show it. He merely continued to sit beside her, looking on at the dancers, while General Maddison tapped out the rhythm of the tango on the side of his glass and looked as if he would like to be among the dancers himself.

No sooner had the tango come to an end and Carla returned to their table than he insisted that she should be his partner in the next dance, and as it happened to be an old-fashioned waltz this particularly delighted him, for he had been dancing waltzes in Simla when she was not even in her cradle. Clive caught sight of two of his tennis pupils at another table and went over to speak to them, and for the first time Virginia and the doctor found themselves seated alone at the table on the edge of the dance floor.

Léon Hanson said suddenly, as if he had been thinking the matter over, "So you don't want to dance with me?"

Virginia gave a little start, looking up at him in a queerly frightened fashion.

"Why should you think that?"

"I don't merely think it, I'm sure of it!" And then, before she could say anything further, he suggested, "But I think we'll forget about that blister on your heel and dance all the same, don't you?"

Mutely she stood up, recognizing that there was no other course open to her. As she had suspected he was a perfect dancer. He held her just as closely as Clive had done, but not a fraction of an inch more closely, and instead of talking as they circled the floor he looked over her head and seemed to be studying the rest of the dancers. Her hand in his was now as cold as ice but, although expecting to stumble a little occasionally and disclose the fact that evenings such as this were an infrequent occurrence with her, she found that she followed his steps perfectly and in fact they moved beautifully together. It was just as if that harmony of thought or instinct or whatever it was that had drawn them together in the first place when they had been, as he had said, on the verge of becoming *real* friends, was exercising so strong a charm upon them physically that united movement was the easiest thing in the world. The only strange thing was that they had never danced like this before.

Virginia began to feel that almost breathless feeling of happiness bubbling up inside her and for the first time in days she knew what it was to come alive again and to be aware of all that life could offer. She even found the courage to lift her head and look up into his face; he lowered his glance and met her eyes and something passed between them that was vital and warm and compelling and made her catch her breath, while unless her imagination was very strongly at fault he did actually tighten his hold about her for a moment. But only for a moment! For just as she was floating in a world of supreme bliss, which had absolutely no connection with the everyday world she knew, the music stopped and the dance was ended and like all the other couples on the floor they wended their way back toward their particular table.

But before they reached it he took her arm and guided her through one of the open glass doors into the hotel garden proper, and she looked up at him with some astonishment. She was still very much shaken by her emotion of the past few minutes and she looked a little pale. Unless the moonlight was deceiving her she thought that he looked rather pale as well, especially about his well-cut lips. But the rest of his features might all at once have been carved out of granite.

"It's quite all right," he told her quickly, coolly. "No one will think it in the least strange that I want to have a few words with you and I'll return you to your friends in a minute. But first I want you to answer me a question."

"Y-yes?" she stammered, coming to a halt in the middle of the tree shaded path and looked looking up at him.

"Does Lisa know that you are dining here tonight with both the Maddisons?"

"Why—why no!" she had to admit, because after all it was the truth, and she saw the icy look of disdain and cynicism that invaded his eyes as they gazed down at her, and trembled suddenly inside.

"I thought so!" The cynicism was in his voice, too, and it was distinctly harsh. "There were moments when I was beginning to be a little misled while Lisa was still here and young Maddison haunted her almost as much as he haunted you, but now it's plain for everybody to see which of the two of you he prefers! He's even persuaded his father to come out and meet you and that's certainly something—especially as the old man is quite obviously completely captivated by you! How soon am I going to be permitted to congratulate you? And Maddison, of course!"

"I don't think I quite—quite understand what you're talking about!" Virginia answered him, speaking in a slow, bewildered fashion, although one thing at least was painfully clear to her and that was that he thought her capable not only of so soon forgetting her sister's departure but of behaving traitorously toward her and deliberately trying to annex Clive! After all that Lisa had gone through and suffered, he thought that Virginia was capable of trying to rob her of the one thing that had really given her courage to face up to her ordeal and that was now a part of her life!

His opinion of her must be low indeed!

"Don't you?" There was a rough note of impatience in his voice. "I think you do!"

Virginia gazed at him as if she was suddenly a little dazed, and indeed the abrupt transition from a dizzy state of happiness to one bordering on shocked awakening had had the effect of making her feel that way. She was conscious, too, of a sick sensation of disappointment; a disappointment greater than any she had ever experienced before. It even prevented her from thinking clearly, for at one moment she could have been certain that that strange, bewildering tumult that had had her whole inner being in its grip while they were dancing had found some close kinship with the look that had flashed into his eyes when he suddenly held her more closely, but apparently she had been wildly mistaken. She had never been more mistaken in her life!

She said a little hollowly; "Well, if I do, I'm not very anxious to talk about it! Shall we go back to the others?"

"Are you going to marry Clive?" he asked bluntly, ignoring her suggestion.

"I haven't thought about marrying Clive, and in any case I

have a job to do at the moment. Won't Miss Spengler be
wondering where you are?"

He bit his lip in an uncertain fashion.

"Then you're deliberately misleading Clive—and that
delightful old gentleman, his father?"

"I only met General Maddison for the first time tonight,
but if you care to think that I'm misleading him you can.
And now I'd like to rejoin the others, if you don't mind!"

"Very well," he replied with sudden stiffness. "And I must
apologize for seeming to interfere in your affairs, but I was
amazed to find you here tonight, obviously thoroughly
enjoying your evening when Lisa only left for home this
morning. I always imagined that you and your sister were
very devoted to one another."

"We are," she told him flatly, "very devoted to one
another." But his opinion of her was so evident that she felt
she could endure no more. She turned and started to walk
back along the path to the hotel and he had no alternative
but to follow her.

Carla Spengler was sitting at their table trying to appear
interested in General Maddison's flow of talk when they
returned and joined the others, but at the sight of Virginia
being escorted by the tall, dark-haired doctor, the blond
singer's lips instantly tightened and her blue eyes gazed with
rather more than her customary coldness at Virginia.

"I'd like to go now, Léon," she said as he sank into a chair.
"I'm rather tired and the floor show is over and it's a bit dull
now."

But nevertheless she smiled very sweetly at Clive when
they said goodbye and she smiled almost as sweetly at General Maddison. If he bored her a little he had succeeded in
impressing her quite a lot, and she was feeling rather vexed
with Léon for absenting himself with that insignificant little
English governess.

Surely now that the sister had gone back to England there
was no reason why he should continue to obey his quixotic

instincts and take such a protective interest in the young woman who was left behind?

She would have to talk to him about it when she got him alone!

VIRGINIA DID NOT ENJOY the remainder of the evening, but for Clive's sake she strove to appear as if she was having a wonderful time, and she must have succeeded for the General continued to think that she was quite delightful and she was a better listener to his anecdotes than that slinky, golden-headed woman with the very beautiful but curiously unsympathetic blue eyes.

If that doctor fellow was thinking of marrying her, it was to be hoped he had the power of putting a little warmth into them sometimes or life for him would be an unenviably bleak affair despite so much physical perfection!

Only Clive noticed that Virginia was making a tremendous effort to appear natural after she danced that one dance with Léon Hanson, and he hoped she had not been unwise enough to become seriously interested in him when there was not a hope on earth that her interest—even if it was returned—would lead to anything satisfactory. Not when it meant entering into competition with Carla Spengler. Carla had told him while they danced that she hoped to be married soon. And there was only one man she was likely to marry and that was Léon Hanson!

So Clive was particularly nice and almost gentle to Virginia, and he thanked her at the conclusion of the evening for helping him in the way she had done.

"Without you to break the ice things might have been tricky," he told her. "But, as it is, I've a kind of feeling that they're going to be all right!"

And Virginia felt she could be thankful for that, at least, for if they were all right for Clive they would be all right for Lisa. It was only for herself that they would not come right!

CHAPTER SEVENTEEN

THE SUMMER PASSED and autumn came to the lakeshore. The colors of autumn were even more triumphant and splendid than those of the springtime; but whereas the pastel-tinted springtime had held out promise of golden days in store, the autumn blazed away briefly like a forest fire and the first chill breath of winter came in with clammy mists that sometimes turned to rain and were at last succeeded by the first fall of snow.

Virginia had never seen such snow before or such a brilliant blue sky when the clouds passed onward, and the sun shone forth again. It was exhilarating and good to be alive in such a world and if everything else had been as wonderful as the weather and the conditions under which she lived nowadays, she would have felt that there was little left to wish for to make life perfect.

But life was not perfect. It was a day-to-day routine of attending to the wants of her two charges and watching them grow more sturdy and fit every day in that healthy atmosphere, of imparting a certain amount of knowledge to their youthful minds, eating and sleeping amidst luxurious surrounding and earning the ever-growing friendly esteem of Mary Van Loon and her husband. The latter, after a brief stay at home, had to make another trip abroad and Mary had a sudden urgent desire to go with him. Virginia was quite capable of making herself entirely responsible for Peter and Paula, and as Madame d'Auvergne had by this time returned from Paris and would be on hand to advise her if necessary, it was finally arranged that Mary should go with Edward. So for several weeks Virginia was alone with

very pleasant evening alone for once in their own home; in
fact he was actually looking forward to it by the time Peter,
with the complete lack of consideration of one of his years
and—Mary would have added—sex, took matters into his
own hands and declined to allow Virginia to progress so far
as the bathroom when the moment arrived for her to begin
her preparations for the evening. In fact, so determined was
he that she was not to leave him that his temperature
suddenly shot up alarmingly, and it was as much as she
could do to still the panic in her own breast as she stood
feeling his hot hands and head and deciding that the
uncanny brilliance of his eyes was positively ominous.

Mary, on her way back to her bedroom after her own
bath, looked in in her sky-blue bathrobe and was about to
warn Virginia to hurry up with her dressing when she saw by
the look on Virginia's face that something was amiss.

"What's wrong?" She went quickly to Virginia's side. She
spoke without seeming to speak into her ear. "Do you think
we should to get Dr. Boulanger?"

"No. But it's no use pretending that I can go out for the
evening because I can't!"

Mary looked really vexed. She bit her lip hard while
Virginia fetched a flannel wrung out in warm water and a
towel, and bathed the invalid's scarlet face and moist,
clinging hands, and then turned the pillow beneath the curly
dark head and spoke soothingly into the small ear. Peter
seemed to relax even as she spoke and a little of the
feverishness died out of his eyes.

"It's simply infuriating," Mary declared, walking away to
the wide window and staring out over the brilliant surface of
the lake. "That little monkey couldn't help catching a chill, I
know, but you've become so indispensable to him that he's
simply not going to *let* you go!"

"Well, I don't really mind." Virginia was actually
speaking no more than the truth, for her conscience had
been troubling her badly all day at the thought of deserting

her most sensitive charge at the time when he needed her most, and she doubted very much whether she could have enjoyed herself at the dance. "These things happen and it's not doing a bit of good getting worked up over them. And if Peter fretted himself into something serious just because I wanted to have a good time I'd never forgive myself."

"I know you wouldn't." But Mary continued to bite her lip. "All the same I do think it's a bit hard!"

"But you and Mr. Van Loon must both go. It would never do if we let Madame d'Auvergne down!"

"I was going to suggest that Edward go and I stay here with you—"

But one glimpse of the antagonistic gleam that instantly came into Virginia's eyes convinced Mrs. Van Loon that such a course as that would never be permitted by her youthful governess.

"Very well." she agreed with a sigh, "but if I do go and anything goes wrong or you're not altogether happy at being alone—although of course you'll have Effie on call if you need her—you must telephone me at once and I'll come immediately and Edward as well. And now I suppose I'd better go and get dressed."

"Yes, do," Virginia coaxed her.

When both her employers had left the house and all was quiet both above and below stairs, Virginia felt she could settle down to her strangely quiet evening. For the radio in the little sitting room that she shared with the children would have to be silent tonight and her only distraction would be a book—if Peter slumbered enough to make reading possible—and the thoughts that she would permit herself of Lisa, at least, having a good time in her lovely new white lace dress, and dancing beneath the fairy lights in the arms of the admiring Clive Maddison.

If Clive had had no serious intentions where Lisa was concerned before tonight, surely he would have then once he had seen her in that dress with her regally poised small dark head and her dark eyes brilliant with happiness.

the children and the servants in the big white villa on the shore of the lake, and for her life assumed a placid kind of unreality because she had no contact with anyone outside the villa save Madama d'Auvergne.

Aunt Héloise was always delighted to have her visit for tea when she could manage it, and the two seemed to get close to one another again as they had been in the days when Virginia had been her guest. There was a difference, however, because they never talked of Léon Hanson. His footsteps never sounded in the tiled veranda when they were sitting comfortably together with flowered cups and the silver teapot on the table between them, and the telephone never once rang to announce his imminent arrival.

Madame d'Auvergne refrained from mentioning her nephew because she had a feeling that Virginia would prefer it that way, but Virginia was always dreading lest his name should suddenly be allowed to crop up in the conversation, and she would hear news of him that would drive the blood away from her heart and make it impossible for her to keep what she was feeling out of her face.

News that he was to be married and that he would be married soon. That was the thing she feared, although she knew it had to happen some day and she was endeavoring to school herself to a condition of mind that would permit her to be almost unaffected by the news when it did finally come.

One other thing she hoped, however, was that she would not be in Switzerland when the Hanson-Spengler engagement was announced, for she had made up her mind to return to England just as soon as she could leave Peter and Paula. She was aware that plans for their schooling in England had already been discussed.

She saw nothing of Dr. Hanson all the time that she was alone at the villa with the children.

By the time Mary Van Loon and her husband returned the

snow had fallen, and they brought a party of friends with them who were eagerly looking forward to winter sports. In order to satisfy the desires of these friends the Van Loons decided to open up a chalet high up in the mountains. It was an exceptionally large and commodious one so the whole party was accommodated, including Virginia and the two children and the maid Effie, who was now recognized as a nurserymaid.

Not far from the chalet was the hotel where Virginia had once lunched happily with Léon Hanson and dined with him not quite so happily the same evening. It was the Hotel Grunwald, and the valley that it overlooked was now a white carpet of snow and a perfect paradise for winter sports enthusiasts. They thronged the hotel in their bright pullovers and caps and scarves, performed wonderful feats with their skis, and never tired of returning up snow-covered slopes and then being precipitated down them again at whirlwind speed that was enough to take any onlooker's breath away.

At nights they danced in the centrally heated small ballroom of the hotel, exchanging their colorful day wear for fashionable evening clothes. The brilliant lights from the hotel windows shone out across the snowy wastes and the music of the orchestra that supplied the accompaniment for dancing went echoing down the lonely Alpine valley where, at the time of Virginia's first visit, the cattle had jangled their cowbells while moving through a sea of blossoms of almost every known hue and the luxuriant green grass had been kissed to emerald by the sunshine.

But now there were no flowers and no cattle. The balcony where Virginia had so enjoyed her lunch was powdered thick with snow, and instead of being overhung by a gaily striped awning that afforded protection from the sun, it was a very popular spot with sunbathers who found that the midday sun under that brilliant sky enabled them to acquire a tan every bit as satisfactory as that that the summer sun bestowed on them.

The Van Loons and their party spent a good deal of time at the hotel and it was on the beginners' slopes surrounding it that Virginia first learned to ski. At first she was quite sure that she could never master the art and she even tried to persuade Mary to let her off attempting it. But Mary merely laughed at her nervousness and assured her that she would quickly overcome it, and as both children took to skis very much in the same manner as ducks take to water, she realized that she would appear fainthearted indeed if she alone of all the party insisted on remaining an onlooker.

Once her initial nervousness was overcome she found that Mary was right and she very quickly became proficient, although, she realized, there was little danger of her becoming an expert.

Before they left the villa she had bought herself a ski suit of navy blue woolen material that effectively kept out any cold, and with it she wore a scarlet cap that suited her so well that Edward Van Loon didn't hesitate to tell her so, particularly when he met her toiling up the beginner's slope with flushed cheeks and brilliant eyes, the two children looking like a couple of vivid elves on either side of her.

And as there was an unattached young man among the party it was not long before she was receiving other compliments, as well, and if she had wanted to have a really good time she could have had it with the young man dancing attendance on her and the children by day and begging her to take advantage of the hotel ballroom with him at night.

As it was, the change of altitude, the brilliant weather, and the sudden carefree life did tend to have a slightly uplifting effect upon her spirits and she wrote home to Lisa to tell her all about the joys of Switzerland in the wintertime.

Lisa was no longer in any sense of the word an invalid and from the reports Virginia received from Cromwell Road she was now practicing hard at her piano again and was happier than she had ever been. This was easily accounted for by the fact that she had just become officially engaged to Clive

Maddison, after a visit to his Buckinghamshire home, High End, where she had been warmly received by the general and his sister, Aunt Hetty who had never forgotten Clive while he was away from home. Clive had apparently taken with zest to farming and was proposing to run his father's five- to six-hundred-acre farm after a brief refresher course at a local agricultural college. He and Lisa planned to get married early in the New Year. Indeed, they had already decided on a date at the beginning of January and this piece of information did not really surprise Virginia for she had known from the moment she first became aware that Lisa had lost her heart—and lost it completely—to Clive, that all her thoughts would now be fixed on the inevitable outcome of falling in love with a man who, fortunately for her, returned her feelings in fullest measure.

No doubt when she was married she would continue with her playing and she might still become a concert pianist. But success would no longer mean as much to her as it would have done if she had never met Clive. It would mean a great deal, but not as much as marriage to Clive.

Virginia thought of Lisa with all the affection she had always lavished on her and hoped above all things that Lisa would be happy. Nothing mattered very much so long as Lisa was happy!

Her own future was a trifle bleak, but for the present she was refusing to dwell upon it. She was trying to keep her mind a blank insofar as the days ahead of her, when she would have left Switzerland behind, were concerned.

But nevertheless Lisa's letter, giving all the details of her engagement and the weekend she had spent at High End, did something to disturb Virginia's carefully built-up wall of indifference—of imperviousness, rather—to events that might be likely to affect her nearly and make her capable of feeling. She definitely did not want to feel anything at all apart from the importance of carrying out her routine duties. Not until she had had a chance to get thoroughly well used to the idea of having to do without something really vital in her life, anyway.

The letter had arrived after lunch and as they had been lunching at the hotel with the children left behind at the chalet in the temporary care of Effie, Virginia was free to seize the opportunity to wander away from her employers and their friends, and read and reread Lisa's impulsive communication in the privacy of a little pine wood at the back of the hotel.

The sun was falling golden about her, finding its way between the rows of straight trunks, and immediately in front of her there was a wonderful view across the whole width of the valley, sloping steeply down to the ribbon of frozen river that wound among great boulders like gigantic lumps of sugar icing. Tiny creatures moved down there, a villager bent beneath the weight of the load on his back, a man with a sleigh, another man—or it could have been a woman—skimming the white waste on a pair of skis.

Virginia sat on a fallen tree trunk, three-quarters of her mind on Lisa's letter, one quarter occupied with the magnificent view. One day in the far distant future she would remember these mountains, tier upon tier of them rising against that perfect sky, the purple shadows on the snow cast by the tall pines drooping beneath their burden of white and the orange light of the slowly westering sun, and she would hardly be able to bear thinking about them because locked up in them would be so many memories.

She sighed raggedly and then gave herself a half-angry shake. Thoughts of this kind led her nowhere and if she permitted herself to think them they had almost a demoralizing effect upon her. She began to feel bewildered, hopeless, lonely, confused in her mind, and she was determined not to feel any of those things. So she stood up and concentrated determinedly on Lisa's letter.

It had to be answered and the sooner the better. Lisa would be looking for congratulations from her more eagerly

perhaps than from anyone else and they must be speeded on
their way as quickly as possible.

So she made up her mind to go back to the chalet and start
writing to her without delay. The others would not wonder
where she had got to for she was reasonably well able to
control her skis these days. The distance to the chalet was
not much and she often returned before the rest of the party,
especially when she had the children with her and it was
important that they should not miss their afternoon rest.

She was always a little nervous about starting off on skis,
but once that rather bad moment was passed she enjoyed the
hiss of the flying snow below her and the sensation of actually flying through space. It was then that she suddenly felt
uplifted, as if all at once she had sprouted wings; her ambitions soared and she wished that the journey from the hotel
to the chalet was far greater than it actually was, or that she
had the skill of those experts who thought nothing of a long
ski run such as she would never venture to attempt.

But today there seemed to be something wrong with her
left ski and one of the straps had not been properly fastened.
Halfway down the slope to the chalet she tried to interrupt
her descent in the way that she had seen Edward Van Loon
do with ease, but all that she succeeded in bringing about
was a heavy fall that ended in her rolling over and over down
the slope, hopelessly entangled with her skis, and coming to
rest finally in a deep drift of snow from which she found it
almost impossible to extricate herself.

It was a most undignified position to be in and moreover
the fall had shaken her considerably. She felt bruised and
battered and every time she tried to grasp at something solid
to get herself out of the drift she merely clutched loose,
crumbling snow and sank deeper into the white, soft cushion
into which she had fallen. She was scarlet in the face and
almost sobbing with frustration and a nervous dread that
she might eventually sink deeper still and become smoth-
ered, when a figure swooped down to her out of the very

sky, or so it seemed, and within a matter of moments she was on her feet and leaning against someone who seemed to regard her with a great deal of amusement, although until she lifted her head and looked into his face she was only able to detect the laughter in his voice as he said, "Have you any idea, I wonder, how funny you look just now? What in the world were you trying to do?"

Anger seethed through Virginia, a kind of anger such as she had rarely felt before in her life and it made her voice shake uncontrollably as she answered, still without turning her head around to look at him, "What do you think I was doing? And if I looked so funny why didn't you leave me and prolong your amusement? It would have been worthwhile entertainment!"

The tears flowed fast and furiously when at last she met his eyes. She could never have explained to anyone, not even to herself, why she should cry like that at a moment when she would have given anything not to, and why it was just as if deep down inside her some floodgates had been opened and the tears poured forth without any volition of hers and certainly without her approval.

It was true that there was a nagging pain in her left ankle, and for a period of time that was actually no more than a few seconds she had been filled with an almost unreasoning panic, but now she was on her feet again and her dignity demanded that she should make light of the whole incident. Certainly when an inconsiderate fate sent Léon Hanson across her path again at such an ill-timed moment she should not have begun to cry like a frightened schoolgirl.

But she could not stop crying and she put her hands up to her eyes to screen them from his gaze. The tears trickled through her fingers, when all at once his amusement abated and he inquired sharply, "Have you hurt yourself? Tell me, how bad was your fall?"

"It wasn't a—a bad fall at all. I simply rolled down the slope."

"But did you twist your ankle or anything like that? Are you in any pain?"

"No, I—yes—no—no, I don't think so!"

Her shoulders were shaking so that he put his arm about them and held them firmly.

"Stop crying!" he ordered.

"I c-can't," she answered, looked at him for a moment with drowned eyes and then found his handkerchief thrust into her hand.

He gazed down at her consideringly, her bright head with its scarlet cap on a level with the tip of his chin.

"If you don't stop crying I'll kiss you!" he threatened and all at once she drew away, gave a little gasp, choked, mopped at her eyes with his handkerchief and then looked up at him apologetically. As if by the miraculous wave of a wand he had succeeded in stemming the flow of tears, and the scarlet that once more invaded her cheeks was this time the result of acute humiliation—although his threat might have had something to do with it as well!

"I rather thought that would do the trick," he murmured and smiled humorously again. Virginia, experiencing a sudden reaction, could not prevent herself from smiling wanly, too.

"I'm so sorry I made such a—such an exhibition of myself!" she apologized. "I can't think why I did."

"Can't you?" He regarded her with a whimsical gleam in his eyes. "Well, if you'll sit down for a moment I'll examine your ankle. I believe that left one's troubling you, isn't it?"

Virginia admitted that it was and he made a careful examination. There was not a large amount of swelling, but the ankle had received a nasty twist.

"I don't think you'll do much skiing for the next few days," he told her, "but there's nothing seriously wrong and certainly nothing is broken."

He was kneeling in the unblemished snow at her feet and for the first time she was sufficiently calm to take in all the details of his appearance. He wore a pale primrose-colored Windbreaker of soft and supple suede, a black scarf wound about his neck, black gloves and black pants thrust into heavy ski boots. He was hatless and his black hair looked like a wing of satin in the sunshine, and his healthy tan was most attractive. When he smiled at her his teeth flashed white in the sunshine, that was becoming moment by moment more noticeably tinged with red, and although his eyes twinkled at her there was none of the hostility she had last seen in them on the night when she had dined with General Maddison and his son.

"I think I ought to apologize to you for feeling inclined to laugh at you," he told her, "but on the other hand, if I hadn't come along when I did I don't know what would have happened to you!"

"Neither do I," she admitted and then abruptly she laughed, too and she laughed almost as hysterically as she had cried. He eased her boot back onto her injured foot and then gently he patted her hand, resisting the temptation to laugh with her.

"I'm afraid you've had a bit of a shock," he said.

"It was my own fault," she told him. "I thought I was a much better skier than I am and I was careless about fastening the strap of my ski. It was a case of pride going before a fall."

"Well, we'd better get you home, hadn't we?"

"I didn't even know you were up here in the mountains," she told him, looking at him with sudden shyness. "Are you staying at the hotel?"

"Yes, I arrived last night, and I've been out on the Edelhorn all day." The Edelhorn was the famous ski run running upward through forests. It entailed a very considerable climb and a quite perilous descent, favored only by fully fledged skiers with a calm disregard for life and limb. He stood up suddenly. "Do you think you can trust me to carry you and ski you down the rest of the slope at the same time?"

"But can you do that?" She looked as if she thought it was quite impossible.

"Of course I can do it."

"But—"

"And since we can't fasten a ski to that left boot of yours there's nothing for it but for me to carry you."

He gave her a smile that was encouraging, essentially friendly and a little humorous at the same time.

"All you've got to do is to put your arms around my neck, hold me tight and leave the rest to me." He put out his hands and drew her to her feet. "That's simple enough, isn't it?"

"If you say so."

He laughed suddenly and his laugh was almost boyish. "I do say so!"

But the moment when Virginia's hands clasped themselves at the back of his neck and he lifted her into his arms was a memorable one for her. Her heart was beating almost painfully with excitement and she was afraid he could hear it since he held her so close. He held her, too, as if she were no weightier than a feather, despite the slenderness of his build. She realized that he was probably exceedingly strong and he was certainly completely fit, which was not surprising if he could spend whole days on the Edelhorn.

Just before they started off he looked down into her face and smiled at her more quizzically.

"All you've got to do is hang on!" he said.

And she closed her eyes and hung on, turning her face almost into his neck while she did so.

When he carried her into the chalet Effie was the only one there to receive them. The two children were still resting in their room and the place was very silent, especially the big lounge where a bright fire burned on the open hearth.

Dr. Hanson made Effie fetch some cold water and bandages and he dealt with Virginia's ankle while the maid stood at his side and obediently handed him anything he required. When he was finished he dismissed the maid and piled cushions at Virginia's back, telling her that she would have to rest her foot for a day or so, but after that it would be quite all right for her to get around on it again.

"Thank you very much for bringing me down," Virginia said, inwardly still thrilled by that rapid descent to the chalet while he had held her closely in his arms and she had clung around his neck. It was one more memory to take back to England with her, but it was the most exciting memory of all those she had collected while she was in Switzerland.

Effie brought them a tray of afternoon tea and he stayed and had some with her. It was almost as if they had got back on the old footing as they talked and even laughed sometimes quite naturally together. When the Van Loons returned Mary was astonished to find him there and very much concerned about Virginia's ankle. She was also concerned because there was to be a grand gala dance at the hotel the following night and she felt it would be a pity if Virginia had to miss that as she had had to miss the dance at Madame d'Auvergne's villa.

"We'll have to get you there somehow," she said, "although I don't suppose she'll be able to dance, will she, Léon?"

"She certainly won't be able to dance," he answered, "but she could look on at the other people dancing if that would amuse her?"

Virginia knew that it would amuse her very much—or it would if it meant he was going to be there and she could look on at him, dancing, talking to other people, or even, perhaps, paying a certain amount of attention to herself! She realized that she was preparing for herself another fool's paradise, but at least since she knew that it was a fool's paradise there could be no harm done. And even if there was any harm in it, it could only be harm to herself!

And it was something to know that Carla Spengler was not staying at the hotel, too, and for just one night, perhaps, it would be rather like those days before Lisa's operation

when she had scarcely realized that she was falling hopelessly in love and life had still held some sort of promise

Mary could not help noticing Virginia's brilliant eyes and
flushed cheeks and she thought to herself, *I wonder...?* Was
it the result of her adventure in the snow, and a sprained
ankle? Or had Leon Hanson anything to do with it?

Oh, I hope not. thought Mary. *I hope not!*

And yet....

There was still no news of an engagement between Léon
and Carla Spengler despite the constant predictions that
there would be one soon!

CHAPTER EIGHTEEN

THE FOLLOWING MORNING Dr. Hanson made a point of calling at the chalet to inquire about Virginia's ankle, and found her lying comfortably in a chaise longue on the wooden balcony, with the two children getting her to read stories to them while they faithfully carried out their aunt's instructions and saw to it that Virginia did not think up any pretext to move.

Virginia, like everybody else, had acquired a deep tan, and at sight of the doctor the blood rose quickly to her cheeks and the damask blush was most becoming. He stood looking down at her with that suspicion of a twinkle in his eyes that she had encountered the day before and she found it impossible to meet his direct gaze for any length of time. She was secretly both flattered and surprised that he had bothered to look in on her this morning, and when he knelt down to examine her ankle and his bowed head came reasonably close to hers she felt as if her breath was suspended, and was sure that he must have heard that quick little intake of it when his cool fingers so lightly touched her injured foot.

"Well, how do you feel about the dance tonight?" he inquired as he looked up at her. "Would you rather be left here in peace and quiet or shall we put you in a sleigh and take you up to the hotel? I've asked Mary and the rest of her party to dine with me tonight and I don't really think we can leave you out!"

"I don't want to be a nuisance to anyone," Virginia replied while the children watched fascinatedly as he reapplied the bandage to her ankle, doing it very neatly and quickly, and then fitted her slim foot into her small velvet slipper. "And if it's going to be any trouble getting me to the hotel—"

"It won't be any trouble," he assured her. "I'll come and fetch you myself and then I'll be sure that you're not accidentally left behind," he said, looking up at her with a faint, attractive laugh in his eyes.

Virginia wanted to meet his eyes—she wanted desperately to meet them but she could not.

"That's very kind of you," she told him, her heart hammering.

"Not at all. We can't have history repeating itself and your missing another festive occasion."

And then he occupied himself in amusing the children until he left, and once again Virginia was surprised to see how good he was with them and how much they seemed to have taken to him although they had seen so little of him. He promised that if they were still there at Christmas when he returned for a longer stay, he would take them on the funicular railway, the little mountain railway with steeply tilted carriages that pulled itself up through the blue pine forests almost to the very summit of the mountain, and they were delighted by the promise. They chattered about him for a little while after he had left and Virginia was perfectly happy to listen to them, for he was a subject she could never hear enough of.

That night she managed to dress herself with care in the black dress, and as the swelling of her ankle had practically subsided she was able to wear her fragile silver sandals with the somewhat perilous high heels. But Léon Hanson had said, quite firmly, "No dancing! You will be permitted to look on at the dancing and that is all!"

But that, she felt, would be more than enough, especially as he was going to fetch her and take her to his dinner party himself.

Mary's eyebrows rose a little when Virginia told her that the doctor was calling for her himself, but she said nothing.

If it was more usual for the host to await the arrival of his guests she did not point this out to Virginia but she went into her room while she was completing her toilet and offered her the use of her most expensive Paris perfume. She insisted also that Virginia wear one of her costly fur coats, a soft and supple mink, as a protection, she said, against the vicious-ness of the night air.

By the time she was ready Virginia knew that she had never looked quite like this before, not even on the night when she had dined with the Maddisons. For one thing there was an excited glow inside her and it was given away by the happy, anticipatory light in her eyes. What she was expect-ing from this evening she could not tell, but she did know that whatever happened after it, at least she would have tonight. She had suddenly become infected with a kind of gambler's spirit, a spirit of recklessness and wild hopefulness that was foreign to her, at any rate lately, and its effect on her appearance was quite marked.

"You look absolutely lovely, my dear!" Mary told her and then, as if she were suddenly touched, she kissed her quickly and lightly on her delicately powdered cheek. "I wish we could keep you with us always!"

Virginia echoed that wish in secret. If only she could stay here in this country always—if only it could become her country!

When Dr. Hanson arrived he offered to give anyone else who might require it a lift in the sleigh, but Mary assured him quite hastily that she had everything arranged, and there was no need for him to take another passenger. He looked at Mary a little quizzically before he helped Virginia into the sleigh and then they started off, the stars like lamps above them and lesser lights shining like lesser stars in the windows of the humbler homes they passed on their brisk, short journey.

Virginia's hands were clasped tightly in her lap to still her excitement, and Léon Hanson looked down at her, a strange little smile on his beautifully cut mouth in that cold, white, unearthly light.

"I do believe," he observed, "that you've been looking forward to this evening. If so, I hope you won't find it dull after all."

"I won't find it dull," Virginia answered, and her voice was so quiet that he said no more to her until they arrived. And then he carried her up the steps of the hotel and into the brilliantly lighted entrance.

The dinner party occupied one large table in the center of the dining room, and the table itself was massed with flowers, the best that the hotel proprietor had been able to procure at fairly short notice. There was champagne; there were other wines and the choicest of food and deferential service from the waiters. Virginia was given a place on her host's left hand and the place on his right was allocated to Mary Van Loon. The young man who had recently become quite openly enamored of Virginia gazed at her completely fascinated throughout the whole of the meal. Dr. Hanson regarded him once or twice with a look of amusement on his face and divided his attention equally between Mary and Virginia, and to a lesser extent among the rest of his guests.

He was the perfect host, with exquisite manners that never failed him, and Virginia wanted to follow the example of the young man who gazed at her and keep her own eyes glued to the man beside her, but naturally she did not do so because for one thing her eyes, she knew, would have been hopelessly revealing.

But the meal was a bright and cheerful one. When it was over the dancing began in the adjoining ballroom and Virginia was assisted to a comfortable couch in the shelter of a palm in a brass-bound tub—how she recalled that other palm in that other brass-bound tub that had protected her from the eyes of the rest of the diners at the Milano on her first night in Switzerland—and each member of the party offered to forgo dances and keep her company. But the host had very decided views on this subject, and he announced that he was going to keep Miss Holt company to begin with, at least, and after that they could all take turns if they wished.

The ballroom looked very gay with its colored streamers and flowers and iridescent lighting, and for a while Virginia remained on her couch with her feet on a footstool. Dr. Hanson provided her with a cigarette and then lay back against the cushions beside her and watched the moving kaleidoscope of color as the couples glided on the polished floor. Virginia lay back against the cushions also and with her shoulder almost but not quite touching his she was more than content to watch the dancers and take no active part in the evening. She felt a little guilty because her ankle was so much better and she was keeping him thus chained to her side, but otherwise she was supremely happy.

The music was soft and seductive and the numbers played were mostly favorites of Virginia's. It would have been wonderful to have been waltzing with Léon, but the next best thing was to have him here beside her like this with scarcely anyone near enough to observe them.

After a time he said, "It's a bit hot in here. This central heating is rather apt to get out of hand at times, and it will be cooler on the veranda. Would you like to go out there?"

"I don't mind either way." But she stood up at once when she saw he was anxious to move and he offered her his arm for support while they made the brief journey to the long closed-in veranda. Here he settled her comfortably on another settee and took his place beside her as before, only this time he did not relax against the cushions, but leaned forward and smoked his cigarette and stared through the big glass windows out at the night.

"You can still hear the music and it's pleasanter here," he observed. Then he turned and looked at her a little curiously. "How are you getting on with the Van Loons? Do you like looking after those children?"

"Oh, yes," she assured him. "I'm very fond of them."

"You seem to manage them fairly well." He crushed out his cigarette in an ashtray and selected another. "Have you any plans for the future?"

She was silent for a moment, wondering why he had asked that question. Then she said, "I'll remain with the children until Christmas, then I'm going home early in the new year."

"I see." He stared hard at the toe of his polished shoe. "You're beginning to feel a little homesick, is that it?"

"Sometimes, yes," she admitted.

"How is Lisa?" he asked.

"Oh, she's doing very well, both physically and at her music. Her old music teacher is very pleased with her and the fingers are quite supple again."

"That's excellent!" he declared.

"But there's something I must say to you!" The thought of saying it made her feel suddenly embarrassed and she sat very upright, with her fingers locking and unlocking themselves in her lap. "My father has written to tell me that you have so far ignored all his requests to submit your account and—and we will all feel much better if you will only do so. After all, Lisa came to you from England as a patient just like all your other patients and—"

"And what?" he asked, smiling at her.

"And you performed a very successful operation on her and we are all very grateful—tremendously grateful!"

"Then surely that is payment enough?"

"Of course it isn't," she replied, infusing into her voice a sudden indignation, because he had no right to believe they were prepared to allow him to operate on Lisa and keep her as a patient in his clinic without charging them anything at all. After all, he was a famous surgeon and although she and her family were not well-to-do, they had their pride like everybody else, and it was not their practice to try and evade payment when they had incurred a debt. "You must see that it isn't! Why, we were complete strangers to you—"

"Tell me why you want to go home after Christmas?" he interrupted her flow of indignation by asking mildly. "Is it because you have really become very homesick or are you tired of Switzerland?" Then before she could answer him he continued, "I'm planning to spend Christmas up here in the mountains myself, and as it's only about two or three weeks away I was hoping you would still be here with the Van Loons and that you would stay on for a while after that. It's much jollier at the holiday season if you're in a large party, and there'll be some good skiing later on when the snow really hardens up."

"I'm afraid I'm not a very good skier," she admitted, recalling her undignified tumble of the day before.

He laughed, looking at her face.

"I could teach you to become a very good skier!"

Suddenly, and she didn't know why she had to do so, she posed a question, "But won't Miss Spengler be coming here for Christmas as well? I expect she's already an expert on skis?"

"Yes, as a matter of fact, she is," Dr. Hanson admitted. "She's quite a brilliant performer. She'll certainly be here for Christmas and her parents as well."

This time it was Virginia who said, very quietly, "I see!"

He regarded her thoughtfully. The lights in the veranda were far dimmer than they were in the ballroom, but they were sufficient to enable him to see that her face all at once had become very small and pale and inscrutable, or so it seemed to him.

He reminded her with a new kind of gentleness in his voice, "You haven't told me yet why you're going home?"

"Because I must," she replied, suddenly feeling rather vague. "Because of the wedding," she added.

"The—wedding?" He shot her quite a startled sideways glance but she did not notice it, for she was staring straight ahead and thinking, *Of course Carla will follow him here and they'll spend Christmas together! Why in the world was I so stupid as to imagine ...?*

Dr. Hanson was grinding his half-smoked cigarette beneath his heel.

"When is this wedding to be?" he asked curtly.

"Early in January," she told him.

"And I suppose you want to go home to begin preparations?"

"We shall have to begin preparations fairly soon—" she was beginning, when all at once it struck her that he must have entirely misunderstood her and that after all it was not surprising, since she had not told him that the wedding concerned Lisa and not herself. It was on the very tip of her tongue to explain to him that it was not she who was getting married when something made her pause. One glance at his face, pale, set and a little hard about the lips, coupled with his admission that he could not apparently go anywhere for any length of time without Miss Spengler following hard at his heels—and how he had managed to snatch this brief holiday he was on now without Carla she could not think, but as he was staying for another two days she might arrive at any moment—suddenly helped her to make up her mind.

It was not a deliberate deception and he would probably find out very soon that he had made a mistake, but for the remainder of this evening there was no reason why she should not gather together the remnants of her pride and deceive him a little. He who had treated her to a kind of cat-and-mouse game of being utterly charming to her at one moment and reminding her at the next that he was not free to be taken seriously! He obviously enjoyed amusing himself with her a little—otherwise why had he threatened to kiss her again only yesterday? But it was Miss Spengler, the beautiful, accomplished, secure Carla with whom he proposed to spend the rest of his life!

She swallowed something in her throat, something like a lump that had risen up in it, and at the same time she shook a little with a sensation almost of anger. Thank goodness for Clive and that dinner at the Milano, which had made it possible for him to believe that she was not altogether unwanted at least! And Lisa wouldn't mind. Lisa wouldn't mind in the very slightest!

"Is this all rather sudden or did you make up your minds before our young friend Clive went home to England?" he inquired with a cold curl to his lips. "Or perhaps discovering that you would have such a pleasant father-in-law helped you to decide?"

"I—"

But it was unnecessary for Virginia to attempt anything further, for Mary came quickly from the ballroom and rallied them both in her cheerful tones.

"We wondered where you two were hiding yourselves! But if you'd like to go and dance, Léon, I'll stay here with Virginia and keep her company. They're playing a tango and I believe you're rather good at it—"

"Yes, do dance, Dr. Hanson," Virginia urged him, and Mary looked from one controlled face to the other with a surprised lift to her eyebrows.

"Very well." He stood up and bowed a little to them both before he left them. "If you don't mind missing a dance, Mary. Perhaps Edward, or that other young man who stared so hard at Miss Holt during dinner, will keep her company for the next dance and you'll be free to take the floor again."

"Well!" Mary exclaimed when he had left them, looking at Virginia keenly. "Is anything wrong?"

"No, nothing," Virginia told her hastily. And then she added, "But do you think I could go home soon, Mrs. Van Loon? I'm sorry if it's going to be awkward but—" she seized thankfully upon her ankle as an excuse "—my ankle—it's a bit painful...."

"Of course, my dear," Mary answered at once and her expression softened. "I'm afraid you're not having a very exciting evening." She could have added that she had thought, however, that Virginia had found all the excitement she either required or desired in sharing a couch in a subtly lit, enclosed veranda with Dr. Hanson, but she did not do so. One glance at the two faces when she had joined them had told her that something was very wrong between them. "As a matter of fact, I was thinking of going home early myself, so we'll go together. If you like, we'll make our excuses now and fetch our wraps."

"So long as I'm not really taking you away—" Virginia demurred.

"Not a bit, my dear. I can do with an early night. Come along!"

They could not find their host, for he appeared to have vanished, but Edward promised to convey their good-nights and their thanks to him. When they reached the chalet Mary said cheerfully, "We'll have an English pot of tea before we go to bed, and if I were you I'd take a couple of aspirin tablets. You do look a bit tired and they'll help to soothe your ankle."

IN THE MORNING Edward took Peter and Paula to the beginners' slopes and Virginia managed to spend a short time with Mrs. Van Loon alone. She had lain awake half the night trying to make up her mind what to say to her, but now she knew what she was going to say.

"I want to go home, Mrs. Van Loon, and I want to go as soon as you can spare me. Today, even, if it could be managed."

"My *dear!*" was all Mrs. Van Loon could say and then she sat deliberately studying Virginia, who was certainly not the Virginia she had been a few days ago. There were smudgy mauve circles under her eyes that told the story of a sleepless night and the eyes themselves were dull and lackluster. She looked a little pinched, too, and very pale, although that might be because her ankle was troubling her.

"I know it's all terribly sudden," Virginia said, speaking quickly and nervously, "but you know that Effie is quite capable of looking after the children altogether now that we've got her so well trained, and in the New Year they're both going to school in England. That is already fixed."

"Yes, but, my dear, I was going to ask you to stay on as a—well, as a kind of companion," Mrs. Van Loon told her.

Virginia rewarded her with a wan smile.

"That's terribly nice of you," she said gratefully, "but I think you only thought of that because you thought I might be hurt. And I must go home. I'd have to go directly after Christmas if I didn't go now, but I'd rather go now if you can spare me."

"Of course, if you feel you must, but all the same—" Mrs. Van Loon looked puzzled. "Don't think I'm trying to interfere," she said gently, "but has it anything to do with Dr. Hanson?"

Virginia was silent for a moment and then she stared down at her hands in her lap.

"Y-yes," she admitted at last, "it has."

"You—rather like him don't you, dear?"

Virginia simply lifted her eyes and then lowered them again immediately, and Mary Van Loon sighed.

"I was afraid something like that was happening," she told the younger woman, "and as I knew there was always Carla in the way, I rather hoped that—well, that you would get over it or that he would have the sense to keep well out of your way. But last night I must admit I rather gathered a new impression about you both and I began to hope that something might come of it after all!" She leaned forward and took Virginia's hands gently within her own. "You're quite sure that nothing *can* ever come of it and that's why you want to go back to England?"

"Last night," Virginia told her, "I let him think that I am going to marry Clive Maddison! Actually it is Lisa who is going to marry Clive; I had a letter from her yesterday telling me all about it. But Dr. Hanson always believed that it was I who was interested in Clive."

"And to save your pride you are prepared to let him go on thinking that?"

"Yes. If only you will help me to keep up the pretence until I am back in England."

Mary Van Loon looked inexpressibly troubled.

"It seems a foolish and dangerous thing to do," she said. "He's bound to find out before very long, and what then?"

"Nothing," Virginia replied bitterly, "except that he'll probably be wholeheartedly thankful I've removed any slight temptation from his path. Please!" she begged Mary. "Please don't say anything to contradict what I've told him until I'm at home, and please let me go at once! I could get the funicular down to Gstahl and take the express from there. And I could fly the rest of the way—I can easily afford it."

"And you won't come back? Not after you've had time to think things over and perhaps realize that they're not so serious after all?"

Virginia shook her head with a mixture of decision and mournfulness.

"No, I'll never come back."

"Oh, my dear!" Mary exclaimed and gave her hands an entirely sympathetic squeeze. "But what am I to say to Léon when I see him, as I'm almost bound to do before he leaves, and if he asks for you?"

"Tell him I—tell him I was recalled home urgently, and that I hadn't time to say goodbye to anyone!"

"But won't he think that rather strange? And what if he wants to know what sort of trouble you were recalled home to?"

"It's hardly any affair of his, is it?" Virginia murmured, and there was something quietly implacable about her that made Mary Van Loon realize that her mind was fully made up and nothing she could say would do anything at all to help her to change it.

"Very well, my dear," she said, albeit reluctantly. "If that's the way you feel then there's nothing for me to do but offer to help you pack. But you must give me permission to let

Madame d'Auvergne know the truth. She had grown very fond of you, you know, and it wouldn't be fair to keep her in the dark. You do see that, don't you?"

"Well, yes," Virginia admitted after a moment of hesitation. And then she sighed rather wistfully as she thought of Aunt Héloise and her lovely orchid-mauve salon. Dear Aunt Héloise! More than anything she would have liked to say goodbye to her and to have thanked her once again for all her kindness.

CHAPTER NINETEEN

VIRGINIA NEVER REMEMBERED very much about that journey home to England. She only knew that it started to rain as soon as they sighted the Channel and that it was simply pouring when they touched down at Heathrow Airport. It was cold, too, raw cold after Switzerland and she shivered as she stood looking about her in the faint hope that someone she knew might be at the airport. But as she had neglected to inform anyone of her arrival, there was no real reason to expect that anyone would be there to meet her.

The airline company's bus took her within a reasonable distance of her home and a taxi conveyed her the remainder of the way. It was Friday and she remembered that on Friday evenings her mother and father always went to the movies, and as it was term time her two young brothers would both be away at school. But Lisa would probably be at home, most likely practicing her piano, unless she, too, had gone to the movies or was spending the evening with Clive. But as Clive was now at his agricultural college that did not seem very likely.

For a moment, when she first rang the bell of the apartment, she was certain they were all out for there was no sound of Lisa's piano and there was also no sign of any light save a dim bulb in the hall. But then footsteps came somewhat hesitatingly along the corridor and Lisa herself opened the door, holding her old blue dressing gown around her and endeavoring to conceal as much of her person as possible behind the door.

"Jinny!" she exclaimed, and ceased holding the dressing gown and threw the door wide open.

"Liz!" Virginia exclaimed and smiled lightheadedly at her. She dumped her suitcase on the floor of the hall and the two sisters fairly ran into one another's arms. They hugged one another delightedly and then stood back to view each other's faces. But Lisa was completely bewildered.

"Why on *earth* didn't you let us know you were coming?" she demanded. "Oh, Jinny, what in the world has happened that you had to take us by surprise like this? Mummy and Daddy are out and it's Betty's evening off, and if I'd been out, too, who would have let you in?"

"I'd have had to camp on the doorstep until you all returned," Virginia told her, trying to laugh as if that would really have been very amusing, although the laugh was such a husky little effort that Lisa was not deceived. "Or, at any rate, until one of you returned."

Lisa said nothing, but drew her into the lounge where she gave a hasty poke to the fire and switched on the big standard lamp that stood just behind their father's favorite armchair. Looking around the room Virginia saw that it was almost exactly as she had seen it last, with the same litter of magazines and library books, a piece of sewing flung down carelessly on a corner table, the television set unused except when the boys were at home, and Lisa's magnificent piano dominating and dwarfing everything else.

It had always been an untidy room, a homey room, but it was now a haven of refuge, or that was the way it appeared to Virginia after her long hours of cold and wearisome travel. She sank down into a chair near the fire and huddled over it, holding her hands to the blaze that sprang up, and Lisa explained why she was wearing her dressing gown.

"I've been trying on a dress," she explained, "one that I bought this morning. It's to be part of my trousseau. Daddy gave me a check last week so that I could start getting things, but if I'd had the faintest idea that you were going to turn up this evening I'd have been all ready to receive you. But, Jinny, why are you here when the last we heard was that you were thoroughly enjoying yourself in Switzerland?"

"I suddenly felt homesick," Virginia told her and Lisa knew that that was only a part of the truth.

"And Mrs. Van Loon agreed to spare you?"

"She didn't particularly want to, but—the children are going to boarding school here in England after Christmas and I would have been leaving them in any case. And I wanted to come home and see you all—I did want to see you all again very badly!" she answered incoherently, looking with a kind of hungry wistfulness in her face at her sister.

Lisa gazed at her in a concerned fashion, for she could never recall Virginia looking quite like this before; not only pale and peaked and travel weary, but with something about her that suggested she was trying to conceal the fact that at heart she was almost numb with hurt. There was a blank look in her eyes despite the fact that the sight of Lisa had acted like a temporary tonic, and a kind of quiver at the corner of her mouth that she found difficult to control, although she was constantly catching her lower lip between her teeth and holding it hard to steady it. She was also trying to smile hard, too, at Lisa, and Lisa thought the smile completely unnatural and altogether unlike Virginia.

She decided that for the time being it would be as well not to press for information on the subject of why Virginia had not even bothered to let her family know she was returning, and began instead to deplore the fact that there was very little in the house to provide a welcome home spread.

"And I expect you're terribly hungry," she said. "But if you'd like to come to the kitchen with me I'll scramble some eggs and make some coffee and we can talk while you're eating. It's horribly cold and raw today, but it's warm in the kitchen—warmer than here because I let the fire get down."

"And you really are able to use your hands again quite normally?" Virginia inquired as she sat at the scrubbed kitchen table and watched her sister busying herself at the stove.

"Oh, quite normally!" Lisa shot her a sudden radiant look. "Isn't it marvelous? And all because of Dr. Hanson! Mommy and daddy say they can never be sufficiently grateful to him, and they do wish he'd send in his account even if it's absolutely staggering."

Virginia started hastily to butter toast while Lisa watched the eggs.

"I expect he'll send it in one day," she observed, wondering whether her voice sounded particularly flat to Lisa. And then, to change the subject, she added, "And you're getting married early in the new year? That's one reason why I had to come home—to help you get together all the things you'll be needing. I simply couldn't let you indulge in an orgy of shopping of that kind alone!"

Lisa smiled at her with warm appreciation.

"Then in that case I'm absolutely delighted you've come home, because shopping for one's wedding is the most madly exciting thing I know and I've been wanting someone like my dear and only sister to trail around with me through the bargain basements! You've no idea the bargains I've picked up already! All sorts of things we'll be wanting for the home, although I expect we'll live with the general after we're married, and he's such an old pet it'll be great fun. His sister's been finding that big house too much for her lately and she says she'll be glad to live with another relative and make way for me as the new housekeeper."

"Then I hope you know something about housekeeping?"

"I don't know much at the moment of going to press, but I will by the time I'm married." Lisa looked so happily confident that Virginia could scarcely believe she was the same Lisa who had lost all, or practically all, interest in life before going to Switzerland. "Betty's teaching me to cook and I've got all sorts of books on the subject."

"But you're still keen on your music?"

"Oh, yes. I shall keep on with that, of course. But naturally it's Clive who comes first now—as he always must and will." Virginia let her talk away about Clive and all their plans for the future, and she did not need anyone to tell her that Lisa was completely and absolutely devoted to the man who in a very short space of time was to become her husband. There was a look on her face when she even mentioned his name that was a revelation to Virginia, who had grown so much accustomed to having a sister who lived only for music. The dull ache of longing in her own heart for a man she would probably never see again in her lifetime made it almost painfully easy for her to understand this attitude. There could be no other attitude when you were in love.

The kitchen clock ticked away the minutes and Lisa went on talking until at last she noticed that Virgina was not only looking white and strained, but that she seemed to be hardly listening. She put it down to the fact that she must be very tired and suggested that as their mother and father were likely to be late she should go to bed, and Lisa would sit up and wait for them and let them know about her return.

"They'll be thrilled to bits to know you're back," she said. "Daddy's missed you terribly."

And Virginia felt glad of one thing at least, and that was that she was home and that on the following day she would see both her parents, and in particular her father, who had always seemed to understand her better than anyone else.

BUT ALTHOUGH HER mother and father gave her a really warm welcome home and Lisa was plainly delighted to have her back, Virginia found settling down at home again the most difficult thing she had ever attempted in her life.

It wasn't that her affection for her own people had lessened while she was away, but other interests absorbed her mind to such an extent that she could think of nothing else. She began to be afraid that all her life she would be haunted by the image of one man; that try as she would she would not be able to forget him, and that the ordinary things in life would remain perpetually without any sort of savor for her.

When Lisa asked her to go shopping with her she found it impossible to work up any enthusiasm for lengths of material or displays of gossamer underwear. Household linens, brocades for curtains, antique furniture, none of these things could hold her attention for long. She followed Lisa from counter to counter, in store after store and felt as if she were being propelled by something purely mechanical, and as if her ability to appreciate anything had died completely. Even the beauty of the Brussels lace wedding veil, which had belonged to their grandmother and which Lisa was planning to wear, passed Virginia by.

When Clive came up from Buckinghamshire he took her and Lisa out and she tried to show some signs of appreciation when he planned a particularly entertaining outing as a mark of his gratitude for that evening when she had dined with him and his father, thereby softening his father's attitude toward him.

They went to a theater, and then on to a nightclub. It should have been a bright and sparkling evening because Lisa seemed so entirely without care and Clive was so proud that she wore his ring, but Virginia had so little life in her that the other two began gradually to be affected by her attitude and the evening was not a success.

When Lisa tried to talk to her about Switzerland and the friends she had made there, Virginia withdrew so determinedly into her shell that Lisa could find out nothing of what had happened to her after she left. But Lisa at least had a shrewd idea, though she hoped against hope that she was mistaken.

Her mother and father began to be anxious about her and to show it, but even her father, close to her though he had always been, could draw nothing out of her. The Swiss experiment had been just an experiment, she said, and now it was over she would take a few weeks' holiday until Lisa

was married and then go back to her old job in the city if it
was still open to her.

A week before Christmas her two brothers came home
from school and the apartment became a hive of preparations for the festive season. Holly and evergreens went up
above the pictures and the hall was festooned with paper
streamers. Virginia had always been popular with the boys
and she did her best to enter into their excited holiday spirit
and to forget this hollow, empty feeling inside her, which
made her despise herself sometimes because she felt that in
not being able to fight it she was lamentably weak. Mrs. Holt
began to make preparations for Christmas in the kitchen
and Lisa helped her, but Virginia's assistance was not the
thing it had been once when she would have enjoyed every
moment of that grand seasonal baking.

When, without making it too noticeable she would get
away from her family, she took to wandering alone around
the streets, avoiding the gaily decorated shop windows. All
that she could think of was the Hotel Grunwald away up in
the mountains where she had once spent a blissfully happy
day with Léon Hanson and the preparations that would be
going on there for Christmas.

No doubt Dr. Hanson was back there by now and Carla,
of course, would be with him. The snow would have hard-
ened and the skiers would be having a wonderful time, and
at night they would dance in the hotel ballroom.

Very likely Carla would persuade Dr. Hanson to
announce their engagement at Christmas, and like Lisa and
Clive they might be married early in the new year. It was
what their friends expected.

Torturing herself in this way it was no wonder that everybody found her changed. But despite the change she did not
forget what was due to people who had been kind to her; she
forced herself to go shopping, and, in addition to presents
for all the members of her own family she bought toys for
Peter and Paula that she dispatched to them in gaily

wrapped parcels, an exquisite hand-painted scarf for Mary Van Loon, and some choice lace handkerchiefs for Madame d'Auvergne that cost her far more than she could really afford, but which of all the presents she was the happiest to send.

For when she had told Léon Hanson that she had grown fond of his aunt she had meant it. She sent rather a wistful little note containing all her gratitude with the handkerchiefs, and Madame d'Auvergne would be touched when she received it.

She went out to post all her Swiss parcels on the same day, a day when the skies were lowering and rain fell steadily. She put on an old raincoat and tied her hair up in a head scarf. When she came out of the post office she decided to walk back to the apartment despite the weather, because all her family had gone out and she would be alone until supper time.

By the time she reached the apartment the rain had found its way even into her shoes and the head scarf was completely soaked. But she was hardly aware of these discomforts and certainly did not recognize them as discomforts, because she was far away in thought with her recently dispatched parcels, following them on their journey to Switzerland.

Just as she reached the top of the steps that led up to the front door of the tall house in which she lived, a taxi drew up at the curb. A man alighted, paid the taxi driver and then turned and looked up at her where she stood on the steps. Something had made her pause and turn her head, and all at once she was certain that she must be dreaming, for those dark eyes beneath the brim of that soft felt hat were so wonderfully familiar.

He moved quickly up the steps until he stood beside her. Without any ceremony he grasped her wrist and dragged her up against him. He said, his voice intensely brusque, "This is where you live, isn't it?"

"Yes." But her voice was a mere thread of sound that escaped her without her own volition.

"Then go inside and change out of those soaking wet things and join me again as soon as you've put on something dry. I'll get another taxi and then we're going somewhere where we can talk."

She was quite sure now that she was dreaming.

"There's no one at home," she said. "Would you like to come in?"

He hesitated for a moment, but for a moment only and then he shook his head.

"No. I'd like to meet your parents later on, but for the present I want to talk to you. Now hurry!"

CHAPTER TWENTY

WHEN SHE JOINED him again she was wearing a camel's hair coat and a little blue velvet cap like a blue velvet leaf on the back of her soft brown curls. She wore hardly any makeup and she looked pale.

Dr. Hanson had engaged another taxi and was waiting to open the door of it for her. As soon as she was inside he gave some instructions to the driver and then got in beside her and closed the door. She seemed to shrink away from him into her corner of the cab.

Dr. Hanson looked out at the rain and the passersby and the general murk and his dark brows met in a frown. He observed rather shortly to Virginia, "It's a very bad climate that you have."

"I know." The taxi was rounding a corner and she had to grip the seat hard to prevent herself being flung up against him. "It's very unpleasant today."

"And yet you walk about in it as if you enjoyed it! Do you make a habit of strolling about the streets in a downpour like this getting soaked through almost to the skin? And is there no member of your family who can prevent you from behaving so foolishly?"

Virginia tried to excuse herself and her family.

"We don't think very much of getting a little wet. And I was wearing a raincoat."

He frowned harder than ever, but he still did not turn and look directly at her.

"It is obvious that you require someone to look after you!"

The taxi gave a second, more violent jolt than the first and this time she could not prevent herself from being flung rather forcibly against him. She clutched instinctively at his thick tweed coat and then gave a little gasp as his arms imprisoned her. His voice spoke roughly into her ear, "I swore that I would punish you for making us both so desperately unhappy, but now that I've got you there's only one thing I can bear to do to you and I'm going to do it now!"

When he had kissed her on the bridge in the little pine wood there had been a certain gentleness about the kiss, although it was also determined; but this kiss contained no gentleness and it not only bruised her lips, but it drew, or seemed to draw, all the breath out of her body. It was completely demanding and there was an unrestrained hunger in it that was no greater than the hunger she had known for him. It rendered her so entirely helpless that all she could do was cling to him with her cold, ungloved fingers while the taxi sped on over the slippery, wet, shining surface of the road. The rain teemed down on all sides of them and the dusk of evening descended like a mantle over London.

At last Virginia's head went back against his shoulder and her little blue velvet cap fell off, but still his mouth refused to leave her mouth and their hearts thundered against one another. The taxi swayed, slowed, jerked almost to a standstill and then went on again, and at last, although very reluctantly, he lifted his head. Virginia gazed back into his eyes, so close to her own, and never in all her wildest dreams had she imagined those brilliant dark depths so filled with undisguised passion and adoring love as they were in this moment of breathless reality.

"Virginia!" he exclaimed in a voice that shook. "Oh, Virginia, my darling, my little love!"

Virginia could say nothing, but the expression in her eyes in that half-lit taxi was more than sufficient to tell him all he needed to know. He drew her head down into the hollow of his neck and his fingers entwined themselves in her soft

brown hair; he whispered to her endearments that shook her
to her very soul, and he kissed her again with a lingering
tenderness that had nothing to do with that first desperate
claiming of her lips.

Virginia put up a shaking hand to caress his cheek and he
caught it and held it against his lips.

"Virginia, *why* did you run away like that and leave me
without any clue as to why you had gone? If it hadn't been
for Aunt Héloise I might not have found out even yet."

"Did she tell you?" Virginia whispered into his neck. "But
she didn't know—"

"Oh, yes, she did! Mary Van Loon told her, for one thing,
and for another, she didn't really need any telling, because
she's always understood you far better than I have! I've
never been able to be certain how you felt, although I've
loved you—adored you—from the beginning!"

A look of complete wonderment appeared on Virgina's
face as she lifted it to gaze at him, and she struggled up in his
arms because this was something she found it almost impossible to believe.

"From the—beginning . . . ?"

"Yes, my darling, from the moment that great, hulking
lump of a fellow swung the door of the dining room back
into your face at the Milano and brought up that bump on
your head. Although I think as a matter of fact, the sight of
you, even before that, sitting alone at that table not far away
from me, decided me that the one thing I really wanted in life
was you and that if it was humanly possible I'd got to have
you! You were so small and adorable and so shy and lovely
that I think I could have swept you up then and there and
defied anybody and everybody to take you from me!"

"Oh!" Virginia exclaimed, breathing ecstatically as she
sank back against him. "And I thought—I thought that it
was Miss Spengler!"

"Carla? Why should you think things like that about
Carla?"

"Because everyone said you would marry her!"

He appeared mildly surprised.

"Carla and I have known one another since our earliest years but I'm quite sure she has never been in love with me, and I know that I have never been in love with her! We are good friends and I hope we shall continue to be good friends, although at the moment she is thinking of marrying a rich American and he will probably take her away from Switzerland. If you had not run away as you did you would have met this American during the Christmas holidays for he will be staying at the Grunwald and perhaps if you saw the two of them together you might agree with me that Carla has never had any serious thoughts of me."

"And you don't mind her marrying another man?"

"*Mind?*" He appeared so genuinely puzzled that the floodgates of her relief were suddenly opened wide. "Why should I mind?"

"I don't know," she admitted, "except that I thought—"

"What you thought," he told her, putting his fingers under her chin and lifting it so that he could gaze at her with all his adoration in his eyes, "was nothing to what I thought and felt when you told me that night of the dance at the Grunwald that you were going to marry Clive Maddison!"

"But I never said I was going to marry Clive! I said I had got to be at home for the wedding—*Lisa's* wedding!"

"Yes, I know now, sweetheart, but you didn't make it very clear to me at the time! And I had planned to ask you to marry me that night! It was why I asked you all up to the hotel—"

"Oh, Léon!" She turned an anguished face to him and clung to him. "If only I had known!"

"That's the first time you've called me by name," he murmured softly, stroking her hair. "And I like the sound of it on your lips! Virginia, beloved, you spent so much time trying to make me believe that you didn't care in the least for me, and if it hadn't been for Aunt Héloise I would be in the dark still. But surely now you can tell me—how much you love me?"

"I love you better than anything else in life," Virginia replied to him with a passionate quiver in her voice.

"And I love you better than life itself!"

The taxi driver had been carrying out his instructions and cruising aimlessly up and down streets that were becoming decidedly monotonous, and all at once he decided to bring the taxi to a standstill. He slid back the glass partition that separated him from his passengers and in a patient voice he inquired without turning his head, "And where to now, sir?"

Dr. Hanson looked down at Virginia, a sudden quizzical gleam in his eyes.

"I suppose it would be a good plan if we went somewhere and had something to eat?"

"I'm not in the least hungry," she assured him.

"All the same, you strike me as being thinner than when I saw you last, and if we can't eat we can at least talk. In any case we can't expect this fellow to drive us over half of London for no specific reason." He leaned forward and spoke to the taxi driver, and when he lay back against the seat again he drew Virginia back into the close circle of his arm. "We're neither of us dressed for the haunts of the fashionable, so I've told him to take us to a little place I know of where we will at least be left in peace to enjoy a good meal if we want one."

"You seem to be very familiar with London," she murmured to him shyly.

"Oh, I spent quite a while over here doing part of my training and I frequently find an excuse to visit London when I can spare the time." He laid his cheek against her hair. "This time the excuse was you, you heartless runaway!"

Virginia was suddenly conscience stricken.

"I've interfered with all your Christmas arrangements! You should now have been at the Grunwald!"

"Never mind my Christmas arrangements and the Grunwald. I've far more important things to discuss with you," he told her.

And when they were seated facing one another in a cozy corner of a quiet little restaurant where the service was excellent and the food even better—if they had felt like food, which neither of them did—and he started to discuss those important things with her, she began to wonder whether she was living in a dream or whether this was indeed reality. For not only did he take it for granted that she would marry him, but he informed her that he was seeing her parents that night to request their permission to marry her without any delay whatsoever.

"But—but that's impossible!" Virginia exclaimed. "Lisa is getting married in January and we'll have to wait—"

"It doesn't matter when Lisa is getting married," he replied coolly. "Her affairs are not really our concern."

"Then perhaps we could be married at the same time?" she suggested, looking at him with adorable shyness because the mere thought of actually becoming his wife was almost more than she could believe.

"Certainly not! Aunt Héloise advised me to marry you the very instant I set foot in England—or the instant I ran you to earth again—and that's what I intend to do! I've very little time to spare and if you think I'm waiting until you've collected a trousseau and invited hordes of relatives to attend our wedding ceremony, then I'm afraid you'll have to stop thinking along those lines!" She was up against his old arrogance, but this time it wasn't merely arrogance; she could tell by the set of his lips as he faced her across the table that his mind was unalterably made up—unless, of course, she flatly refused to have anything to do with his arrangements! But when he looked directly at her and placed one of his hands over hers where it rested on the white tablecloth and she felt the strength and vitality of it, she knew that whatever he decided she would agree to without raising any opposition of a really obstructive kind. "You do want to belong to me, don't you? And I can't altogether trust you, as you've run away from me once!"

"I'd never run away again," Virginia told him and the glow of love in her eyes was more than sufficient to convince him.

His own eyes softened miraculously. They seemed to caress her.

"We'll set whatever machinery we have to set in motion and be married within the next few days. The fact that it's so near to Christmas doesn't make any difference. We'll spend a couple of nights in Paris on our way home and if you want to go shopping you can go shopping where you can get the kind of things that an adorable young woman like you ought to wear! I don't approve of old raincoats and soaked head scarves," he said, frowning at the recollection of the way she had looked when he first caught sight of her that afternoon.

Virginia smiled faintly.

"You would if you had to spend all your winters in England."

"Well, you will spend your winters in Switzerland!" He leaned across the table to her and his voice was urgent, "Virginia, I love you—I love you! I want you in my own house and I want to have you under my eye forever and always!"

Virginia could barely answer him. Her face was rosy with color and her eyes were misted with happiness.

"Oh, Léon!" was all she could say.

CHAPTER TWENTY-ONE

MR. AND MRS. HOLT, the boys and Lisa were all back in the apartment when Virginia took Léon home for the first time. Lisa was washing her hair in the bathroom and she was thrown into a state of the utmost flurry and excitement when she heard voices in the hall and peeped out to see her sister—a new sister this, transformed by happiness and with all her gloom of the past days and weeks utterly vanished—introducing to their parents the man who had given Lisa back the use of her hands.

Lisa did not stop to dry her hair properly. She dressed hurriedly and joined everybody in the lounge, which as usual was comfortably untidy, but warm and homey after the wintry conditions outside. Dr. Hanson looked whimsically at Lisa as he took her hand and she gazed at him a little reproachfully, for after all he had cast Virginia into the depths of unhappiness, although at the present moment she was quite obviously radiant.

"Do you think you'll approve of me as a brother-in-law, Lisa?" he inquired.

Lisa suddenly smiled.

"I think you'll be a very useful brother-in-law to have," she told him, and then turned to Virginia and hugged her. "Oh, darling, I'm so glad!" Virginia was her old Virginia, smiling and cheerful and content. "But I suppose this means we're going to lose you?"

Mr. and Mrs. Holt were quite overwhelmed. They were filled with gratitude that they were most anxious to express to the man who had done so much for Lisa, and to meet him unexpectedly like this was a real pleasure. But that he should want to marry Virginia—and marry her almost immediately—took their breath away. Virginia was her father's favorite daughter and he gazed at her fondly as he saw how openly happy she was, but it shook him that she was going to be whisked away from him again just when he had hoped she would in time settle down to her old life once more. At the same time he realized that the man she had set her heart on was a man to be proud of as a son-in-law, and he could certainly never wish for a better husband for her than one whose reputation was already established, who could offer her an enviable position as his wife, and who, despite his quietly autocratic ways, exercised so much charm that it even made itself felt on the boys, who had been inclined to gaze at him with awe until they decided all at once that he was not merely a "sawbones" who had done great things for Lisa, but a prospective brother-in-law with something about him they could honestly approve.

Despite the fact that he and Virginia had already made a pretense of eating an unwanted dinner, Dr. Hanson agreed to stay to supper with the family, and after that he spent quite a while closeted alone with Virginia's father in his little study. And when they presently both emerged Virginia's future was settled for her and Mr. Holt opened a bottle of champagne he had been keeping for Christmas and insisted upon toasting the pair who were to be married so soon.

It was an evening to remember and Virginia knew she would remember it all her life, just as she would remember that afternoon when, utterly downcast and without any hope for the future, she had returned from dispatching her Christmas parcels and found the one man who counted above all others alighting from a taxi outside her own front door. Her sensations on meeting his eyes for the first time were imperishable.

It was close to midnight when he departed, and Virginia went with him to the door of the apartment. He had booked a room at a hotel not very far away and they were to meet again the next day, but she hated to see him go. She stood within the close circle of his arms, her face upturned to his, as he whispered his good-night against her lips.

"We'll meet again tomorrow morning—early!" he said. "And after that it won't be more than forty-eight hours before you will never have to say good-night to me anymore."

Virginia's eyes were starry with happiness and the subdued light from the hall lantern shone down upon her and let him see how much those words of his meant to her.

When she opened the door for him at last they discovered that the rain had ceased and the stars were quite bright over London. Virginia looked up at them and thought of the stars shining down over Aunt Héloise's garden and of the shimmering surface of the lake which that garden overlooked.

"Dear Aunt Héloise!" she murmured suddenly. "I do really long to see her again."

"As a matter of fact she wants us to stay with her for a few days," he told her, gently stroking her cheek "Until you've had a chance to look over my rather masculine establishment and see what, if any, alterations you would like to make to it."

"She does?" Virginia sounded excited. "That will be lovely!" And in her heart she knew that it would be more than lovely. Aunt Héloise's villa—*and* Léon...! "But I don't suppose I shall want to make many alterations—perhaps not any at all—to your house. What little I saw of it I thought was very nice indeed. And if you like it *I* shall like it!"

"Will you, my darling?" But he smiled at her a little whimsically. "I wonder whether you will say that ten—twenty—thirty years from now?"

She looked up at the stars again, dreamily.

Ten—twenty—thirty years of stars in the lake!